A VALLEY TO DIE FOR

A VALLEY TO DIE FOR

by

Y. B. McKenna

Dales Large Print Books
Long Preston, North Yorkshire,
BD23 4ND, England.

British Library Cataloguing in Publication Data.

McKenna, Y. B.
    A valley to die for.

    A catalogue record of this book is
    available from the British Library

    ISBN   1-84262-209-9 pbk

First published in Great Britain in 1995 by Robert Hale Limited

Copyright © Y. B. McKenna 1995

Cover illustration © Prieto by arrangement with
Norma Editorial S.A.

Published in Large Print 2003 by arrangement with
Robert Hale Limited

Dales Large Print is an imprint of Library Magna Books Ltd.

Printed and bound in Great Britain by
T.J. (International) Ltd., Cornwall, PL28 8RW

*For my husband
and daughter*

ONE

'Boonetown up ahead,' Hayden, the stage driver bellowed, glancing downwards in the general direction of his two remaining passengers.

The township in question had sprung up some time during the previous five, maybe six years, spawning an untidy collection of individual dwellings. It etched the skyline just inside the border of New Mexico where it touched on Arizona territory. In fact some of the town's inhabitants couldn't quite decide whether Boonetown was in New Mexico or in Arizona and that particular dispute regularly raged hot and heavy during the course of various nights' drunken discussions. In latter years the town had acquired a certain order, most notably with the building of Jefferies' large hotel. This establishment in time served to mark the centre of Boonetown with all later construction becoming, as it were, mere satellites circling around it.

Both stage occupants, for different

9

reasons, received their impending arrival in Boonetown with heart-felt relief. Lizabeth FitzMaurice felt as if she had been travelling in the bouncing stage just about forever. She wasn't sure she'd ever recover! She leaned forward on hearing Hayden's words, eager to catch a glimpse of the town but fell backwards in an undignified heap as the driver pulled down hard on the reins.

'Whoa, horse,' he roared, 'damn it, damn it, whoa up there.'

Lizabeth muttered some rather unladylike words beneath her breath, glaring potently through the stage ceiling at the oblivious Hayden.

'Howdy, Taggart,' he yelled. Lizabeth hurriedly set about rearranging her errant petticoat, her face warm with embarrassment. She stilled on hearing the rider's name; the colour in her cheeks deepened becomingly and then receded, leaving her deadly pale. Her companion also seemed startled on hearing Hayden yell out, but recovered his composure more easily. He peered through the window with studied care, his face still and without expression.

Hayden had swung the stage alongside the rider whose name was the cause of such un-ease among his passengers. 'Howdy, Hay-

10

den.' The latter glanced upward and grinned in a friendly fashion. 'You made good time.' Hayden grinned roguishly and shook his head. 'Where's Slim?' Taggart added, indicating the vacant place beside Hayden uptop the stage.

'Damn fool went and fell through a roof just afore we set out from Dry Flats; broke his leg.' Hayden spat his disgust. 'Anythin' happenin' round these parts,' he continued, dismissing the luckless Slim with a shrug, 'since I was last up?'

Taggart lifted his hat, wiped his brow with his forearm. 'Ain't been around for near on two months myself.' He squinted, silently watching Hayden steady the team. 'Been deliverin' T.T. horses down to the fort.' He replaced his hat, drawing his mount aside. 'Best let 'em critters on.' He indicated the team. 'Might meet you in Clancy's later for a beer, maybe.'

'Good idea.' Hayden waved and gave the straining team more reins. Taggart covered his mouth and turned his head aside to avoid the worst of the inevitable dust.

Lizabeth studied Taggart eagerly. She had not expected to find him so easily and was unprepared for the effect of encountering him so unexpectedly. She still felt the same, and somehow it still hurt her to look at him. She had almost called out to him, but something had made her hesitate and the moment had passed. Perhaps he would not be pleased that she had followed him here to Boonetown. That possibility had not struck her before and, with the thought, she found her resolve, her sureness failing. She closed her eyes momentarily as fear swept through her. When she next opened her eyes she found herself for perhaps the first time, meeting her companion's empty gaze full on. She had never met his kind before but, nevertheless, she knew him without having met anyone at all like him and she was suddenly, inexplicably afraid.

For some reason she found herself remembering the conversation she had inadvertently overheard at the stage's last stop. Two men had been discussing her companion. Seemed his gun was for hire, payment in advance, and he was one of the best in the business. Rumour had it that he had already killed ten men. Lizabeth took that with a pinch of salt. Rumour had a way of exaggerating things. But still, she couldn't get away from the fact that the boy was most likely coming to Boonetown to kill someone.

She looked away from him afraid of what he might read in her face and wrapped her arms around herself, shivering despite the heat. She was glad to have finally reached Boonetown, for many reasons, none of which she could have articulated then.

Taggart came into town maybe ten minutes behind the stage. Boonetown hadn't changed much in his absence, Jefferies' big white hotel still dominating the main street. He paused to watch the stage's two passengers alight. Something about the woman caused his glance to sharpen. She seemed familiar. He squinted against the sun, his brow furrowed. 'Lizabeth?' he said aloud, and frowned. Damn it, he had told her not to come, wasn't the time. He couldn't be sure though, not with the sun in his eyes. Still, it was mighty unlikely, there was no reason for her to be in Boonetown. He dismissed the notion, kneeing the grey-coloured horse towards the livery stable.

He dismounted stiffly, arching his back to relieve some of the ache, before ducking his head into the water trough. He wiped the excess away with the palms of his hands oblivious to the red streaks of water and dust which stained his shirt.

He stilled then, lifting his head as if to sniff

the air. He was suddenly conscious of danger. Taggart living as he did on the edge, could recognize the smell of danger, almost taste it. A tall, lean man he had something of the wide-open spaces about him, with something deep and still inside him. He raked thin, brown fingers through hair bleached almost white by the Western sun and glanced surreptitiously to his left. His eyes narrowed dangerously as he replaced his hat slowly, his movements careful and in the open.

The stranger who had so unsettled Lizabeth, the man with the boy's face and the dead eyes, studied Taggart with unmistakable intensity. The latter could not fail to realize the implication of the tied-down guns worn by the other.

'You're Taggart,' the younger man stated, in a flat voice. There was silence so still that Taggart could almost hear him breathe.

'You're Billy Taggart, ain't you?' the other repeated in the same flat voice. He pushed himself out of the shadows as he spoke, and now stood maybe four feet from Billy. Taggart did not turn.

'Depends on who's askin',' he spoke softly, securing the grey's reins to the hitching rail with a slip knot.

14

'I heard the stage driver call your name.'

'Reckon I am Taggart then if'n you say so,' the other replied softly, teasingly. Billy straightened then, turning slowly to face the speaker, all his movements executed with an inherently dangerous grace. His quick glance assessed his adversary. He smiled whimsically. His own travel-stained duds compared poorly with the other's fine black broadcloth. The youth's shirt, in spite of the recent stage journey, had somehow retained its white, bright appearance.

'Listen kid,' he said aloud, 'I'm just back from a long trip. What with Indians and the damn sun, I ain't in no mood for games. Draw against me and I'll most likely have to kill you. Maybe you best run along afore this gets out of hand. I don't want no trouble, you understand?'

The kid's eyes merely glinted like twin pieces of ice. He was arrogant, very sure. This cowpuncher was nothing to his way of thinking, a nobody. He snapped his fingers metaphorically. In his mind's eye he had already blown him away.

Taggart squared his shoulders, straightened the guns on his hips. 'Your call,' he said, so low the boy almost didn't catch the words. For a moment he hesitated, arrested

15

perhaps by something in the other's brooding face, an unexpected darkness of spirit thinly masked by the quiet exterior. Inexplicably, fear ran her fingers down his spine but, like a moth to a candle flame, the boy couldn't resist.

The plain truth was that he craved the excitement, nothing more, nothing less. Holding the life of another in his hands was the definitive power. He was almost a god then, giving and taking life at his personal discretion. He stepped back about ten paces, hands hovering just above his guns. There was the familiar tension, the hot flood of anticipation, the singing along his nerves. The youthful face suddenly seemed infinitely older. The dead eyes were bright and feverish, bordering on a kind of madness.

He watched and he waited like some small black vulture in his neat suit and white shirt. He was unaware, except perhaps marginally of the suddenly deserted street, the absolute silence of the previously bustling town. The air crackled as both men faced each other. The dice was thrown that one should live and one die. Their shadows were long and narrow on the deserted street.

Was all that he had accomplished to end here, Billy found himself thinking, on this deserted street, in a cowtown too much like all the other cowtowns he had travelled through?

The boy's hand flashed down then, the gun leaped from its holster. All thought fled as Billy too drew his weapon.

The sound of gunplay was loud in the silent town.

TWO

Taggart didn't know it that day as he cleared leather but it was merely the beginning. Before summer's end many others were also to find their lives irrevocably changed as the violence escalated. In Zack Hale's case the changes had already begun.

Zack, patriarch of the Hale Clan, was a tough, wily old timber wolf. He had stood well over six foot in his youth. The passing years though, and the trouble he had had to shoulder of late, had succeeded in stooping him a little. Some folk he reckoned, in spite of his family being temporarily homeless, would even consider him lucky. He did have him a roof over his head, unlike some he could mention, and he did have some mighty loyal friends. Still, no gettin' away from the fact, wasn't his own roof and that riled him. Charity, that's what it amounted to, don't matter how well intentioned the kindness. If'n he hadn't Jason to consider, he'd have refused outright. Don't matter what the circumstances are, should never have allowed that damn Jim Taylor to persuade him to accept temporary accommodations on the T.T. Being prideful, Jesse had accused him. 'Course he was prideful; a man had a right to his pride, was all he had left now that Saul Jefferies had taken his ranch.

Zack figured on getting that ranch back someday; he'd outwit Jefferies somehow even if it killed him – or Jeffries! He'd wait, he was good at waiting; everything had its cycle, its time, and he'd wait.

Should've killed the damn landgrabber when he'd had the chance earlier that mornin'. Had 'im dead to rights almost from the first moment he and his men had come a-ridin' into the ranch yard. From his vantage point uptop Taylor's loft he could have picked off any one of 'em anytime he'd taken the notion. Zack had kinda hoped something would start so that he could have had a legitimate reason to blow Jefferies right off that fine bay stallion he rode. Zack spat violently, a heavy scowl creasing his weathered features. Just one squeeze of his finger, that's all it would have taken. Hold his breath, take aim and squeeze real easy...

However, to his acute disappointment, Taylor had somehow managed to defuse the situation. Sure, Jefferies had come ridin' in, all puffed up like a damn turkey afore Thanksgiving. But he wasn't foolin' Taylor none.

'I want your ranch, Mr Taylor,' he started off smoothly. 'I'm prepared to make you a generous offer.' Taylor's eyes had narrowed slightly in that way he had.

'Sounds mighty like a threat, Mr Jefferies,' he'd replied mildly enough, but his face was kinda hard.

'Take it as you please,' Jefferies had ground out. It was obvious to Zack that Taylor had gotten under the other man's skin. He bared his teeth in glee as he watched the tempered colour come and go in Jefferies' face.

'Just remember,' he continued, 'no two-bit rancher is going to stop me getting what I want, and make no mistake, I want this valley.'

Hell, Taylor, he just grinned that slow, lazy

grin of his. He didn't show it none, but Zack knew him well enough to figure Taylor was gettin' mad as hell. 'That's what I like,' he said then, kinda soft, 'plain talkin', cards on the table, spit it right out.' He laughed ironically. 'We'll make a Westerner of you yet, Jefferies.' Zack saw the grip on his rifle shift just a mite. 'So,' he continued in that soft voice, 'we all know how things stand now, don't we?'

'I'll make it worth your while,' Jefferies tried again. He hadn't cottoned on to the situation at all, much to Zack's disgust. Hell, any fool knew wasn't nothin' gonna tempt a man like Taylor to give up his share of this valley. Too many dreams and too much sweat rolled into it. Round about then Zack had felt mighty inclined to just let fly from the loft he was gettin' so exasperated. Still, Hank Jaeckell, one of those riding with Jefferies did provide diversion of a kind. The damn fool should never have tried drawing his gun, not with the chips stackin' up as they were. He'd barely cleared leather, when Zack's bullet spun him right round, catapulting him to the ground.

'Wasn't no call to go shootin' Hank like that,' his brother, Ben, kinda whined. Zack didn't see him dismounting none to help his

20

injured kin. The coward just wiped his nose with the back of his hand and sat his horse. Zack was a little put out, he'd have liked a chance to rid Boonetown of ole Ben!

For a time an explosive silence had prevailed. Taylor's rifle hadn't shifted its steady aim from Jefferies' mid-region and Jefferies' riders eyed him like wolves. Jefferies, well he chewed over the situation some, digestin' this unexpected turn of events. It was obvious he wasn't quite sure what to do exactly. Then, as if tiring of the whole charade, Taylor had seemed to decide it was time to take some decisive action, to end it for good and all.

'This here valley ain't for sale,' he bit out, as the final echo of Zack's shot died away. 'Ain't for sale now, and not never. I reckon you can take it that I speak for all three partners of this valley. It ain't for sale. You got that, Mr Jefferies?' His expression had become aloof and bleak, unmistakably hostile. He drew a deep breath and gestured with the rifle. 'Reckon you'd best gather up them dogs of yours now and move on out, off this property.' Jefferies spluttered. Taylor ignored him, continuing with a faint grin, devoid of amusement, 'Right now.'

He watched them with strained patience,

the anger very close to the surface of him. 'Reckon you got maybe five seconds 'till I give my boys the word to start shootin'.'

'You wouldn't dare,' Jefferies spluttered furiously.

'Mister,' Taylor replied, 'you're trespassin'.' He frowned. 'One, two, three...'

'This isn't the end of the matter,' Jefferies bellowed imperiously. 'You'll sell, mark my words, you'll sell...'

'Four, five...'

'Damn you,' Jefferies flung over his shoulder as he turned his horse, jerking viciously on the bit. The animal lunged forward. By the time he'd hit his second stride, horse and rider were in full gallop. Zack fired one or two shots in their general direction just by way of encouragement. It gave him a dubious kind of satisfaction. Taylor glanced upwards towards the loft and grinned thinly.

'Lucky,' he called in an undertone, not turning his head, 'you'd best saddle up, make sure our visitors leave the valley. Don't want no more surprises today.'

The door behind Taylor opened immediately and a tall, lanky youth emerged. He grinned irrepressibly, his whole face alight with a sort of careless energy, all his movements reflecting the same quick exuberance. 'Lucky,' Taylor's voice halted him, 'don't try nothin' fancy now, you hear, just make sure they leave.'

The young man's grin widened. 'Me?' he exclaimed in injured tones, his eyes wide with mock innocence. 'Somethin' fancy?'

Taylor watched him spring into the saddle of a fine-looking sorrel gelding which was tethered close by the main corral. 'Why he's gotta always ride that damn bronco I ain't never gonna understand.' The sorrel was half-wild, with a mean streak. If he'd been a man, he'd have been hanged long since!

'Guess there's just somethin' 'bout that critter appeals to Lucky,' Jesse, Taylor's wife said, as she came to stand by him on the porch. They were silent for a moment.

'Reckon we've got trouble comin' Jess,' Taylor said flatly, after some moments. 'Jefferies now, he ain't about to let go, not the way he wants this here valley.'

She leaned against him. 'We can hold out, Jim,' she replied steadily. 'You know this valley is near impossible to take if'n we all stick together.'

He smiled faintly, squinting into the sun. 'Like a dog with a bone ain't you, Jesse, just refusin' to let go.' He laid an arm lightly across her thin shoulders.

'Ain't never lettin' this valley go,' she replied in a fierce voice, 'not after all we did to earn it.' She bit her lip in a worried way. 'You reckon Taggart'll be all right in town,' she burst out in less assured tones, 'what with Jefferies all riled up and all? He should be back from deliverin' them horses any time now.

Her husband hushed her. 'He can take care of 'imself, you know that, always could. Besides,' he added, rather hopefully, 'it'll be over long afore he gets back, you'll see.

THREE

They continued to stand in the shade of the porch overhang, looking out across the valley. It could still amaze them that they, together with Taggart had built this empire.

In the beginning they had individually owned little, some saddle horses and their gear. Top hands in any outfit, they had gambled on a notion to break in a herd of the wild horses still roaming free in the south-west.

24

Those hardy little mustangs were much in demand as cow-ponies. They could turn on a dime, endure rough terrain and were generally fearless. They had what most cowboys acknowledged as cow-sense. Descendants of the Spanish horses brought to America by Hernando Cortés, they ran in packs like wolves and were readily taken by anyone fast and smart enough to try. The three friends were just desperate enough to succeed.

With cash accumulated over several seasons, the three had purchased their valley and named it, for obvious reasons, the Treble T. Taylor's big black stallion went to stud with a zeal which exceeded even their most optimistic aspirations. Back then, they had put their personal brand on over a thousand acres of good graze and perhaps another thousand acres of scrub.

The valley, with its abundance of water was the heart of the T.T. Somehow it had succeeded in binding them to it then, and would most likely continue to hold them captive, perhaps forever.

'Have to go into town for supplies,' Taylor broke the silence, shading his eyes to look eastwards perhaps in the futile hope that Taggart might at any moment top the rise from that direction. Jesse followed his gaze and she frowned. 'I'll keep 'im out of trouble, never you fear, Mrs Taylor.' Jim patted her shoulder ineffectually.

'Yeah,' she replied in a tight way, 'but who's gonna keep you out of trouble?'

He didn't reply, but stepped off the porch in silence. Jesse's frown deepened and she quickly followed him. Her movements were jerky with tension. She heard Taylor sigh audibly which didn't improve her temper, but nevertheless, he shortened his long strides so that she could fall into step alongside him.

'Our provisions are near clean out,' he reasoned now, picking up the threads of an obviously ongoing conversation. 'Ain't got no choice 'ceptin' to go into town; you know that. Besides,' he continued, 'Taggart is due any day now and he might be needin' help.'

She shook him ineffectually, her fists curled. Despite her efforts to be reasonable, to soft-soap her husband, she found herself rapidly losing the battle with her quick temper. There was an irresistible brightness about Jesse even in anger, an effervescent quality that mirrored the vivacious enthusiasm and warmth she positively exuded. She was by nature, quick-tempered, reckless, a creature of charm and curiosity. She was, moreover, immeasurably caring of those she loved. She was not conventionally beautiful, but there was something undeniably lovely about the thin, pointed face with its overly generous mouth that Taylor could never resist.

'I'll take Lucky along, if'n it makes you feel easier.' He made the concession grudgingly, smiling a little. There was a softness in his eyes as he looked at her.

'Take Killian too,' she insisted stubbornly, pressing her advantage ruthlessly, her voice coaxing.

'Maybe,' he replied soothingly.

She stamped her foot imperiously, forgetting her advantage. 'Damn you,' she yelled, 'you take Matthew along as well.' Despite himself, her husband felt a grin stretch across his face. Try as he might he was finding it increasingly difficult to maintain any semblance of determination. This wife of his was so small and so fierce. He could never deny her when her slanted eyes sparkled as now.

'You sure look pretty when you get all fired up,' he remarked irreverently.

She glowered, almost speechless. 'I ain't,' she snapped, referring to his compliment, her voice rising. 'I ain't, and you know it, so you best save that damn sweet-talkin' for when I'm in a mood to listen.' Immediately regretting the sharpness of her tone, she reached out, taking his hand in a light grasp, running her mouth lightly across its back.

'Please, Jim,' she repeated, her voice softening. His expression was full of regret, but resolute.

'I can't, not even for you, Jess,' he replied in a tone she recognized as final. Her anxiety increased alarmingly. She jerked away violently, but he caught her to him. 'Jesse, I gotta go, we both know that. How long you think we'd hold this here valley if'n we was to let every Jefferies that comes along frighten us so we become prisoners in our own homes?' She held her head to one side, her eyes narrowed. 'I'll be damned first 'fore I let that happen,' he continued. 'This is our home, and I ain't about to let no Jefferies take it away from us, leastways not without a fight.' He scowled. 'Listen Jess,' he burst out, 'don't you think if there was any other way, I'd want to take it?'

'All I'm sure about, Jim Taylor, is that you and your damn pride is gonna get you killed,' she yelled. 'What do you expect me to do if'n Jefferies kills you in town? How you figurin' on protectin' this here ranch then?'

'He ain't gonna do nothin' of the kind,' he retorted. 'You're lettin' that imagination of yours run wild again, that's all. The man made me an offer for the ranch, I turned 'im down, nothin' more than business. Jefferies ain't gonna kill me over that; he's a business man, not some hired gun.

'No,' she agreed in a shrill voice, 'he ain't no hired gun, but I'm damn sure he knows a lot of 'em. Running 'im off like he was some vermin ain't exactly standard business is it?' She glared fiercely. 'Don't talk to me like I was some fool, don't know nothin'.' She took a deep breath. 'And don't you take that tone with me neither.'

Taylor threw her a quizzical look. 'What tone might that be?' he stalled.

'That patient tone, like I was deaf, dumb and blind, and female to boot!' Her eyes sparkled. 'I can still figure some.'

Her husband fell silent, his expression unrelenting. 'Let's get all this out in the open,' Jesse pressed in a more reasonable voice. 'Jefferies just ran off the Hales to our north. He'll be needin' water. We're the nearest water and he knows we control the springs around these parts, so he wants the valley.' She held up a warning hand as her husband attempted to interrupt. 'Yeah, yeah, he used legal means to take the Hale spread. That don't alter nothin', he still stole it. Just happens we ain't got no mortgage, so he can't foreclose like he did with Zack Hale. Don't reckon he'll come offerin' a deal again, so that leaves us plumb in the middle. I reckon, he'll come with all guns blazin', and I don't think he's the kind cares who gets trampled in the rush neither, long as he gets what he's after.' She looked her husband straight in the eyes. 'How'm I doin' so far?' she said, in a dry voice.

He considered lying outright, but he never could lie to Jesse. Instead, he pulled her to him roughly and she laid her auburn head against his chest, suddenly weary, all the fight deserting her. 'Couldn't live,' she whispered into his shirt, 'if'n anythin' was to happen to you; couldn't bear it.'

'First sign of trouble, I promise I'll high-tail it out of there, ain't nothin' gonna happen to me.'

She pushed him away. 'You just be sure you do run,' she retorted, her expression speaking volumes.

'Sure, I promise to run like hell,' he threw back over his shoulder, laughter in the words. There was no answering laughter. He halted then, head down in mock defeat. 'I give up,' he muttered, still laughing. 'Anythin' for peace. I'll take Killian along this trip like you want.'

She waited.

'And Lucky,' he added resignedly.

FOUR

In the wake of Jefferies' undignified retreat, Zack had climbed down to the floor of the barn. He admitted himself just a little ashamed of his bitterness, justifiable as he felt it to be. To ease his mind some, he had set to harnessing the buckboard, anticipating Taylor's trip for supplies.

When Taylor came looking for the buckboard a little later he threw the older man a rather ironic glance. 'Don't need to ask if you know how things are shapin' up,' he remarked, pausing to stroke the nose of each horse in turn.

'You just be sure to keep your eyes peeled,' Zack replied. 'Don't be fooled none by that soft look of Jefferies; he ain't to be trifled

31

with, you hear?' He searched in his vest for his wad of chewing tobacco. Jesse didn't allow no chewing in her house, and he was careful to respect that rule. Still, a good chew helped a man think things out.

'Reckon on takin' Killian along,' Taylor said, gathering up the reins.

Zack nodded, chewing industriously. 'Lucky's up there by the South Pass seein' 'em boys off. Reckon you ought to take 'im along too. He's a mite wild, but one of the best of my boys if'n you find yourself in a tight corner. Might be some fightin' needs doin' 'fore you leave town.'

Taylor grunted as he climbed on to the buckboard. He settled himself, released the brake. 'Hell, folks around here must think I ain't able to figure nothin' for myself. You're the second person in as many minutes givin' advice.' He scowled good-naturedly, cracking the reins across the backs of his team, and the buckboard, with its sole occupant left the barn, gathering pace.

'What's your damn hurry?' Killian hollered, racing from the bunkhouse just as the buckboard tripped past. Catching Zack's commanding nod, he raced to leap on the back before Taylor really picked up speed.

Lucky was waiting for the buckboard

when they cleared the South Pass. 'Howdy,' he yelled cheerfully. 'Reckon you're goin' into town. Can I ride along?' He threw the question at Taylor, urging the sorrel alongside, assuming an affirmative response.

'Seen Pa headin' up towards Dead Man's Mesa, checkin' things out I reckon, just in case more trouble comes. Mighty careful, is Pa.' He reined in a little, as the gelding tried to break into a canter. 'Pa and me,' he rushed on without drawing breath, 'we could hold that there pass easy. Take no time at all to build us a shelter back yonder. Nobody could get into the valley if'n we didn't want 'em to.'

There was actually some validity in Lucky's proposal. Rimmed securely on almost all sides by the mountains, there was an air of impregnability to the valley. There were animal trails of course, but for a man these were highly dangerous and nigh on impossible to negotiate. They also required intimate knowledge of the valley, something to which few outsiders were privy.

'Even one man alone up there, with a rifle and a good supply of ammo could hold that pass,' Lucky declared, turning in the saddle to gauge the reaction of his companions. The sorrel took the opportunity to take the bit between his teeth. His rider was momentarily diverted from his thoughts by the ensuing struggle. 'Best ride 'im ahead some, give 'im a gallop, maybe take the oats out of 'im some.'

He quickly left the buckboard behind, as the sorrel relished his relative freedom to the full. Nevertheless, the team were a well-matched pair and they moved right along. Their harness jingling with the swinging motion, sounding for all the world like church bells heard muted in the distance.

The summer meadows were lush and brightly decked with flowers that morning. The sky overhead was an eggshell blue with the odd white cloud chasing through the blueness. It was very peaceful. Taylor found it incomprehensible that on such a morning all their talk should be of preparation for what amounted to a range war when all was said and done.

'You reckon Lucky's idea might be worth considerin'?' he spoke reluctantly, as if unwilling to shatter the peace. 'If we was to close off the North Pass, put a guard on the South, you reckon Jefferies might get tired of waitin'?' He was thoughtful for a moment. 'Leastways we'd be safe from any attacks while he considered.'

Killian took out the makings, holding the leather thongs of his tobacco pouch in his teeth. He lit up before he replied, watching the smoke curl upwards in a pensive way. 'Maybe,' he agreed, 'but don't you go pinnin' no hopes on Jefferies lettin' go that easy. He'll keep a-comin', you mark my words.'

A hard expression crossed Taylor's face. His hands clenched on the reins. 'Hell and damnation,' he exclaimed. 'Maybe we're all goin' off half-cocked here. Jefferies ain't fool enough to want a range war on his hands. Hell, nobody wants that kinda war.'

His companion turned away slightly. His profile against the backdrop of mountains was grim. 'There'll always be the kind don't care,' he said in a flat voice. 'Men like Jefferies'll start any kind of war, long as it meets their ends. Don't you know that yet, Jim?' Taylor frowned, not sure how to respond.

'Sometimes,' Killian continued, 'I get to thinkin' there ain't nothin' exceptin' hatin' and dyin'.' He closed his eyes then and nestled into a corner of the buckboard seat. Jim glaced once in his direction, but said nothing. He flicked the reins and the team broke into a fast trot.

They had anticipated some degree of difficulty in Boonetown, but the nature of that trouble was not what they had expected.

When the buckboard finally arrived they found the street unusually deserted. There was an anxious hum in the air which didn't escape the trio. Taylor and Killian exchanged a puzzled look. Lucky drew the sorrel alongside. He swung his rifle free of its scabbard, saying nothing.

'What the hell's goin' on?' Killian muttered to no one in particular, articulating what each was thinking. He glanced around the empty town. He too reached for his rifle which lay at his feet. He checked the loading mechanism from habit. 'Somethin' ain't right, that's for damn sure. Lucky, you ride on over to that there store, see what's happenin'.'

Lucky yelled and banged for at least five minutes before the bolted door of the store indicated by Killian opened by the merest crack. A thin, obviously very nervous voice called out, 'You fellers best take cover for a spell, there's trouble down by the livery stable.'

Lucky jumped from his horse and stepped quickly to stand by the door, leaning inwards the better to hear the nervous thread of words. 'What kinda trouble?' he asked impatiently. There was no reply forthcoming. 'What kinda touble,' he reiterated, banging on the door. There was a faint shuffling sound and the crack widened a margin or so.

'Gunfight,' the voice continued. 'Some kid and that Taggart from the Treble T.'

FIVE

Even Lizabeth would find herself unwittingly embroiled in the events of that summer. Having determinedly put aside the discomfiture of seeing Taggart so unexpectedly, she was determined to look upon her arrival in Boonetown in an optimistic light. She had certainly welcomed the meagre shade of her parasol on vacating the stage. The full force of the New Mexican sun had hit her like a resounding slap.

First impressions of Boonetown, however, were proving rather disappointing. Taggart had led her to imagine something much more progressive than the reality before her indicated.

It was actually a relatively young settlement, still struggling to establish its own identity. It boasted a single main street with several minor side alleys, a large goods-store, a large and gaudy saloon-cum hotel, a small but industrious livery stable and finally, a small but growing population. Lizabeth found herself searching eagerly for the schoolhouse with its promised accommodation. She could locate no building which could possibly be identified as such.

Glancing around, she discovered her companion of the stage, unwelcome as his company had been, had disappeared. Having assisted her safely to the sidewalk, the young man had deserted her, probably while she was otherwise engaged watching Hayden throw her few precious belongings unceremonially into the dust at her feet!

She turned now to face the large, white, rather imposing building in front of which the stage had halted. It dominated the town and carried the name, Saul Jefferies, in large lettering across its front. She stepped back hastily as Hayden flicked his whip and the stage swung away leaving her to wonder uncertainly what she was now expected to do. She made a rather futile attempt to wipe the worst of the trail from her person, shaking her skirts, coughing as the dust threatened to engulf her in a cloud.

'Where the hell is Saul Jefferies?' she muttered to herself. 'He knew I would be arriving on this stage, so where is he? I'm tired and dirty and dusty, and just about fed up with this whole adventure. Damn Billy Taggart, and damn his pride too.'

'Ah, Miss FitzMaurice, welcome, welcome,' a voice boomed from the top step of the white building, as if in answer to her thoughts. 'Saul Jefferies at your service, so sorry to be late, business you understand.' The astonishingly handsome man decended as he spoke, and Lizabeth quickly rearranged her mutinous features into more pleasant lines. He extended both hands, surrounding hers in an excessive display of welcome, his smile wide and pleasing, his teeth unbelievably white. 'You had a good journey, I trust,' he continued. Lizabeth could only nod, overcome by the sheer presence of the man.

'Come, let us find you some refreshments.' Again, she could only manage to nod. She noticed that his hands were beautifully manicured and that there was no dirt beneath his nails. For some strange reason that cheered her. 'Perhaps you would

39

prefer to freshen up a little before we dine,' he said solicitously, as she hesitated further. He glanced down at her travel-stained appearance. 'Jackson, the lady's bags if you please.' He nodded to the man waiting patiently by the hotel entrance.

'Come along then,' he said extending his arm to her. He waited while Jackson complied with his instructions, before again indicating that she should commence the climb upwards to the hotel's entrance.

'I have my recommendations here, Mr Jefferies,' Lizabeth managed to speak at last, 'if you care to look them over.

'Later.' He waved away the suggestion. 'I am sure all is in order. You have taught school before, I take it?' he added as an afterthought.

'Why, yes,' she replied, rather surprised, 'of course.' She paused to draw breath. 'Although I feel I must emphasize, not recently. I have been a guest of friends at the fort for the past six months or so. Perhaps you know them, Lieutenant Washington and his wife, Louise?'

'Ah yes, charming couple, charming.'

She glanced quickly at him, but his face was bland, expressing nothing other than a pleasing agreement that the Washingtons were indeed charming. She frowned.

'I was extremely sorry to leave,' she was stung for some inexplicable reason to add, 'but your advertisement for a schoolteacher ... and other reasons...' Her voice trailed off. She was immediately ashamed of her ill-temper.

'Our need of a schoolteacher, yes indeed,' Jefferies obviously felt obliged to say. 'Well, as you see,' he continued, 'our town does not yet have a proper schoolhouse, but this establishment' – he indicated the imposing white building behind him – 'is quite comfortable.' Lizabeth smiled palely. 'We hope to have the schoolhouse completed quite soon. Work has fallen behind, some trouble with local ranchers, but I'll soon have that matter sorted out.'

She licked her lips, determined to regain her composure. 'A range war?' She raised her eyebrows. He frowned, studying her with a certain sharpness.

'No, no,' he inserted quickly, 'wherever did you get that idea; nothing quite so dramatic, just some local ranchers who are too stubborn for their own good. Nothing for you to worry your pretty head about, I do assure you.'

She glanced at him with a pert look. Pretty

head indeed! she thought silently.

During the entire exchange, she had been increasingly aware of the silence of the town, the absence of people walking the sidewalks, the random abandonment of horses and wagons. It was rather eerie.

'Is Boonetown always so quiet?' she asked, glancing around. Before her companion could reply, there was the sound of a shot, followed by a second, and suddenly as if by magic, the town came to life. People rushed from doorways, gushing round Lizabeth and succeeding in separating her from Jefferies. She found herself being swept along in the surge of people, her struggles to resist totally inadequate.

The throng, having reached the pinnacle of its fever, just as suddenly came to an abrupt halt. Being taller than most, Lizabeth was afforded a clear view of the drama at the heart of this behaviour. She recognized Billy of course. For some reason she was acutely aware of the lazy curl of smoke coming from his gun and of his fingers clenched round the handle.

Looking up she found him staring at her, his face pale, his eyes bleak, without recognition. For a split second she was stunned, then she realized that he didn't actually see her at all. His eyes were blank, seeing only the young man he had just killed.

Taylor and the Hale brothers rounded the corner of Main Street just moments after Lizabeth. They pushed through the gathering as Billy Taggart reholstered his gun.

In the final outcome only death had won. In that instant there was nothing save a movement of hand, a confusion of sound. When the gunsmoke cleared there remained of that moment only a brief, ragged rent in the fragile fabric of eternity. The kid's eyes stared into the blue sky, seeing nothing. Perhaps he wondered where all the splendour and glory had gone; who can say?

Billy pushed through the crowd. He had ridden a long way that day. He was tired. The red dust of New Mexico clung to him like an unwelcome second skin and his eyes ached from looking too long into the burning sun. After more than two months' absence, his heart yearned for home, not for this blood-letting.

'Know 'im from someplace maybe?' Sheriff Tom Lawson reached Taggart before his friends from the T.T.

'Nope,' Billy replied shortly. 'Never laid eyes on him 'fore he called me out.' The sheriff studied the toes of his scuffed boots for a long moment.

'Reckon we'd best have us a little talk,' he said, nodding in the general direction of the jailhouse.

'Anythin' wrong, Sheriff?' Taylor's voice interrupted. He glanced first at the sheriff and then towards Taggart.

'Seems like a case of self-defence to me.' He glanced again at Taggart. 'You all right?' he queried.

Taggart grinned palely. 'A mite shaken, but it'll pass.'

Tom Lawson searched his pockets for his pipe before remembering that he had dropped it on to his desk when first informed of the gunfight. 'Everythin's fine,' he inserted quickly, seeing Taylor about to bristle up like a gamecock. 'Reckon near everybody in town saw the boy call Taggart out. Ain't no charges bein' made.' Billy grunted non-committally, raising one eyebrow slightly. He glanced sceptically towards Taylor.

'Just want to have a talk with Billy here, and the jailhouse is more private, that's all.'

Taggart stiffened. 'Ain't nothin' Jim can't hear,' he said, in a tight voice.

Jim laid a hand very lightly on Taggart's arm. 'That's fine, Sheriff,' he said. 'Don't bother me none. We'll be around,' he added, for Taggart's benefit, 'when you're ready to head out.' He drew him aside a little before he left, saying in an undertone, 'Got plenty to fill you in on, but guess it's waited this long it can wait a mite longer.' He straightened his hat, glancing with slightly narrowed eyes in the general direction of Saul Jefferies' large white hotel. 'You just watch your back,' he muttered meaningfully, and turning he rejoined the Hale boys, who were waiting by the buckboard.

SIX

'My goodness,' Lizabeth exclaimed, 'what on earth was that all about, do you think?' She turned to address the remark to her companion. There was a strange expression on Jefferies' face which puzzled her. For a moment he studied Taggart and Tom Lawson as they crossed the street heading towards the jailhouse. He turned his attention to her with an effort.

'I fear that kind of display is becoming all too common on the streets of Boonetown,

Miss FitzMaurice,' he replied, his face now creased in concern. 'It's exactly the kind of thing the more respectable members of our community, men like myself, are trying to eradicate.' He smiled at her. He really was quite an attractive man when he smiled, she found herself thinking.

'Advertising for a schoolteacher was certainly not the first step, but I do believe one of the most important we have taken so far in our campaign for law and order.'

She acknowledged the compliment with a slight nod of her head. 'But surely there's law in Boonetown?' she queried in some surprise. She watched Taggart for a moment, as he disappeared into the interior of the jail in the company of Tom Lawson. Becoming aware of Jefferies' rather oblique look, she dropped her eyes, but not before he had identified the source of her interest.

'Lawson, he isn't really up to the job. A good man, I warrant, but not what Boonetown needs to bring law and order to its streets.'

'And the man with him?' she asked casually.

Jefferies frowned. 'Taggart,' he gritted out. 'Nothing but a trouble-maker. He's the kind who seems to invite this kind of thing.' He straightened his shoulders in an unconsciously self-satisfied gesture. 'I plan to have an election, or rather...' he amended quickly, 'the town council plan to hold an election within the month to elect a new town sheriff.'

She glanced at him and smiled faintly. 'Of course you obviously have your own idea as to who might be the better choice,' she could not resist suggesting.

'But of course,' he agreed smugly, oblivious to the irony behind her tone. He smacked his lips. 'I have someone in mind.'

'But of course,' she said softly.

They said nothing further on the subject, each were silent for some moments, as, deep in thought they retraced their steps towards Jefferies' hotel building. 'It's certainly big,' Lizabeth muttered, looking upwards to the rather grand entrance at the top of the stairway, leading she discovered, into an equally grand lobby.

'I'm glad you like it,' Jefferies beamed. 'It's modelled on some of the finest hotels in Europe.' Lizabeth took a deep breath, glancing around at the abundance of richness which was freely lavished on the interior of Jefferies' hotel. Luxurious velvet-covered seats were artfully arranged in the wide lobby, their rich deep-red pile echoed in the matching drapes which hung from ceiling to floor. She wasn't sure what to say as she preceded her would-be employer across to the desk, her feet sinking into the plush carpet which covered the entire area and led upwards, covering a staircase which, she could easily agree would not be out of place in the finest palaces of Europe.

'It's wonderful,' she breathed at last, her eyes wide in her dusty face. 'I've never seen anything quite like it.' She grinned. 'It's certainly different to what I was used to at the fort.'

He returned her smile. 'This way.' He directed her up the palatial staircase. 'I've arranged for you to have a room on the second floor while arrangements for the promised school accommodations are being sorted out.' He glanced into her face, his eyes compelling and inviting all at once. She suddenly found her pulse racing. 'You see,' he said softly, his breath fanning her cheek, 'I haven't forgotten what was promised.'

She smiled gratefully, if a little breathlessly. 'No indeed,' she replied, 'you've been most kind.'

'Telegram. Telegram for Mr Jefferies.'

They both paused, turning slightly towards the source of the voice. 'Excuse me,' he said with a faintly apologetic wave of his hand, 'but I've been expecting some important news.' He descended the stair quickly, surprisingly light on his feet. Lizabeth took the opportunity to study him. He was a little shorter than she, but seemed taller somehow, with thick black hair and a classically handsome face. He was obviously well educated, his manner was, to say the least, cultured. By his own admission he had travelled widely, certainly as far as Europe. All in all her first impression was pleasant, perhaps more than pleasant. Jefferies seemed well spoken and charming. Surely any girl would be pleased to make his acquaintance and, judging by the admiring looks directed towards her host even now by several of the female guests, there was ample proof of his popularity.

Yet, despite her undeniable attraction to Jefferies, she found herself remembering the silken touch of hair bleached blond by the sun. Even then if she closed her eyes she could visualize long tapering fingers with New Mexico dirt beneath the nails!

She shook the errant thought aside, returning her attention determinedly to the man below. He had by now been joined by another. The newcomer's appearance was in direct contrast to Jefferies' gentlemanlike apparel. The former wore the cowboy's inevitable levis and plaid shirt, and he twisted a worn stetson nervously round and round in his hands. Jefferies was obviously very angry. Now and then he poked the unfortunate cowboy with his forefinger as if emphasizing some point. Lizabeth saw him glance several times towards the jailhouse and she frowned.

Almost without being aware of having done so, she retraced her steps down the stairway. She was within earshot of the two men before either had noticed her approach. 'Damn fool,' she overheard Jefferies say through gritted teeth, 'you're a damn fool.' The cowboy tried to say something in his own defence, but Jefferies continued in the same flinty tone, 'I've just lost near five hundred dollars because of your incompetence. Five hundred dollars, and for what, for nothing.'

Jefferies' back was towards Lizabeth, but the cowboy must have caught some movement of her grey travelling dress. He gestured to Jefferies with his eyes and the latter turned quickly, his face momentarily harsh.

Lizabeth smiled with admirable *savoir-faire*, assuming an apologetic expression.

'I'm so sorry, Mr Jefferies,' she said softly, almost purring, 'but perhaps I could ask a bellboy to show me to my room.' She glanced downwards at her person. 'I'm hardly attired for such grand surroundings, and you are so obviously busy that I feel guilty for having already taken so much of your time.' She had by now extended her smile to include the cowboy. He shuffled a little, nodded his head and then kept his eyes resolutely downcast. Introductions were conspicuous by their absence.

Finding that Jefferies was openly scrutinizing her, Lizabeth tilted her head, adopting a glacial expression. She raised one eyebrow rather quizzically. 'My room, Mr Jefferies?' she said very gently. 'If you please.'

Her host acknowledged the request, clicking his fingers loudly. Several bellhops materialized as if from nowhere, their young faces shining with eagerness. 'Take Miss FitzMaurice to room fourteen, second floor,' he instructed the taller of the group, 'and take care that she has every comfort.' He slipped a dollar bill into the youth's hand.

'Yes, sir,' the latter almost shouted, a wide appreciative grin splitting his face from ear to ear.

Jefferies turned then towards Lizabeth, who had continued to smile in a determinedly grateful fashion. 'Again, I do apologize for abandoning you in this manner,' he said with a resumption of his charmingly cultured tones, 'but business calls.'

Lizabeth gathered her skirts, her head tilted in an unconscious challenge. 'Not at all, Mr Jefferies,' she muttered. 'I fully understand. You've been kindness itself.'

She followed the bellhop up the wide and winding staircase, unknowingly showing a very shapely turn of ankle beneath the raised hem. Jefferies' eyes followed her, a wolfish gleam in their depths as he skimmed her shapely figure in the tightly fitting, grey travelling dress, lingering on her hips as they swayed slightly from side to side.

'Do you think she heard anythin', Boss?'

Jefferies' eyes were still on Lizabeth's retreating back. 'No, I don't think so,' he replied absently, 'and, even if she did, what of it? I can handle Miss FitzMaurice.'

SEVEN

Tom Lawson poured two mugs of strong coffee from the blackened pot which bubbled perpetually on the pot-bellied stove in his office.

He opened a drawer in the scarred desk which occupied more than its fair share of the floor space, and produced a bottle of whiskey with something of a flourish. 'Sit down,' he invited, gesturing towards the empty chair across from his own behind the desk. 'This may take a while, might as well get comfortable.'

Taggart obeyed in silence, reaching across to take the offered coffee without comment. His interest piqued despite himself, he took a long draught of black coffee before placing the mug on the floor by his feet. 'Somethin' happened while I was gone that maybe I should know 'bout?'

'You recollect the Hales?' the sheriff began, bending to top up his own coffee. He held out the pot towards Billy, who shook his head a little.

'Sure,' Taggart replied when all was comfortable again. 'They're our nearest neighbours to the north, meet 'em at church socials and such like. Ole Zack and the boys often come a-callin' on the ranch. Somethin' happen to 'em?'

The sheriff took two quick mouthfuls of coffee, swallowing loudly. 'Jefferies bought 'em out,' he said, in his usual blunt fashion. 'Can't prove nothin' of course,' he continued, 'but there was somethin' not just right 'bout that. The bank just upped one mornin' and foreclosed on their loan. Reckon you can guess the rest. Jefferies bought the mortgage from the bank, gave Zack Hale two days to come up with the cash, or get out.'

Billy drew in a sharp breath. 'Hell, Zack ain't got that kinda money,' There was a pause. 'Them boys worked that spread for near on seven years, it was just beginnin' to show good; couldn't you have done somethin'? Stopped it some way?'

The sheriff threw him a hard look. 'Don't you figure I would, if'n I could?' he exclaimed. 'But I gotta stay within the law; I gotta uphold the law, and there weren't nothin' I could do 'cept issue a warrant to see 'em off that ranch.'

Billy's eyes slipped away from his companion, but not before Tom Lawson had glimpsed the cynicism etched there. He frowned with displeasure.

The sound of boots thudding on the sidewalk outside the window filled the lengthening silence. Both men waited while the sound faded before resuming the conversation.

'What just happened out there,' Billy spoke first, 'reckon it had anythin' to do with the other?'

'Some of Jefferies' men were boastin' as to how they was goin' to take the T.T.,' the sheriff answered indirectly. 'Reckon, from studying Jim Taylor's face when he came to town, that Jefferies did make an offer?'

Billy grinned. 'Reckon he did; sure hope Jim ran the son of a bitch off the property.' His grin faded quickly. 'We could be havin' trouble with Mr Jefferies,' he continued, an edge to his voice. 'Just so you know, it ain't of our askin'.'

Lawson didn't flinch. 'Ain't gonna make no difference if'n trouble starts.' He paused. 'Jefferies figures on holdin' an election come next month, gonna vote in one of his own men as sheriff. Ain't gonna be no law in Boonetown then 'ceptin' Jefferies'.'

'What you figurin' on doin' 'bout that?'

'Ain't what I'm gonna do,' Lawson replied softly, 'it's what I've done already. I've had my suspicions 'bout Mr Jefferies for sometime now. Sent off some wires by way of an enquiry and I've come up with some mighty interestin' facts 'bout how he gets his money.'

Taggart grunted. 'Enough to put 'im away?'

Lawson grimaced. 'Hell no, nothin' that'd stand up in court, not yet. What we need is proof and that's where you come in, Taggart. Then I can use the law to our advantage 'stead of his.'

Taggart leaned forward. 'He ain't gettin' the T.T.,' he interposed in a fierce voice, an unpleasant expression on his face, 'law or no law.'

He contemplated briefly what a man like Saul Jefferies could do to a valley rich as the T.T.: strip mine it for its valuable metals; kill the graze; leave it naked to be ravaged by the elements; cut down the pines to sell as lumber to the railroad, destroying the shelter belt. The soil would wash away with the first rains. All that careful labour, all those dreams laid desolate before the greed of one man. Didn't bear thinking on!

Jefferies was already wealthy beyond Taggart's wildest dreams. He owned the saloon and hotel, the general store, and the biggest chunk of ranch land in the whole territory. Taggart couldn't figure what else a man could want.

Over the years, Jefferies had, with growing interest followed the progress of the T.T. ranch. He had seen it establish itself as one of the finest and most respected horse ranches in the territory. He was genuinely impressed with evidence of its carefully planned breeding programme. To own a Treble T bred horse was fast becoming something of a status symbol hereabouts. The combination of thoroughbred and mustang cross certainly produced a unique animal, both tough and fast. Only recently the T.T. had successfully bid against Jefferies' own spread further up-state, to secure a particularly lucrative contract supplying the army with mounts. Failure, in any guise was distasteful to Jefferies and in this instance served to further establish the T.T. as worthy of acquisition.

Billy stood up suddenly overturning his coffee mug, not noticing. He banged a fist savagely on the desk top before Tom Lawson. 'Jefferies figurin' on runnin us off,' he ground out, 'well, he's gonna have some fight on his hands, that's for sure, 'cos we ain't givin' up that valley.' His face was stern, forbidding and Tom Lawson studying him, thought that a man like Taggart, with so much to fight for, would be a worthy adversary.

'Don't want no trouble in my town, you hear?' He felt obliged to issue the warning.

Billy threw him a hostile look. 'You're tellin' the wrong side, Tom, best tell Jefferies. He's the one startin' all this, not me and not the T.T. You best remember that.'

The cowboy was like a cornered cougar, pacing the room's length. He made Tom Lawson nervous. 'What happened to the Hales?' Taggart stopped his pacing abruptly.

'Stayin' out on the T.T. for a spell, livin' in your bunkhouse I heard.'

Taggart grunted. 'Don't figure on Zack stomachin' that for long. He's a damn proud man.' Lawson pushed some papers aside locating his pipe beneath them. He took his time filling it from a battered tobacco pouch. He ensured it was drawing to his satisfaction before he next spoke. 'Nope, he's only out there 'cause Jim persuaded him that Jason needed a secure place to stay, and that all the boys needed to be together. He figured Zack was doin' the T.T. a favour, helpin' to protect it, now that Jefferies is throwin' his hat thataway.'

Lawson blew smoke in a lazy fashion towards the ceiling. 'Taggart,' he began, 'I want to deputize you. I want you to go down into New Mexico, listen and poke around some, get me proof that Saul Jefferies is supplyin' Indians with bad liquor and guns. When I get me that proof, I aim to put Mr Jefferies away for a long, long time.'

He glaced out the window, a frown between his eyes. 'He ain't gonna destroy my town, not if I have anythin' to say 'bout it.'

EIGHT

Lizabeth continued up the stairs following the bellhop as he led the way to her room. Her face was thoughtful. She wasn't quite sure what to make of Mr Jefferies. Having reached the first landing, she paused. 'Mr Jefferies' office,' she queried lightly, 'which door is it?'

The boy glanced at the first door to her left. 'That's Mr Jefferies', ma'am.' He eyed her in open speculation.

She smiled. 'I've an interview coming up, for the teaching position, and it may take place in that room.'

He shrugged his shoulders. 'School,' he murmured distastefully, 'ain't nothin' school can learn me I can't find out workin' here in the hotel. Got money in my pocket and ain't gonna waste my time readin' and such.'

'Teach,' she corrected automatically. 'Ain't nothing I mean, there isn't anything school can teach me.'

He grinned. 'That's what I say too, ma'am?'

Lizabeth wasn't really listening. She could hear the muttered murmur of voices coming through the wood of Jefferies' office door. She didn't recognize either voice of course, but one in particular was temptingly clear. She listened, catching some of the words. 'Not good enough ... valley ... if necessary...'

Lizabeth stepped a little closer to the door, bending her head in her effort to hear more. 'Move the men into position first thing in the morning,' the speaker continued. 'No more slip ups, you hear?' Lizabeth drew in her breath sharply. She glanced towards the boy. He too had paused, and was watching her with a strange expression on his face.

Lizabeth instinctively knew that the conversation might prove important. She wasn't sure exactly how, but if nothing else, it certainly corroborated everything she had gleaned since her arrival concerning the unrest in the town. She bit her lip, glancing at the bellhop.

It was becoming more and more apparent that she could not accept the position of schoolteacher. But how could she possibly remain in Boonetown if she did not, and that was the sole purpose of coming in the first place – to remain?

During their time together at the fort, Taggart had told her much more than he had realized of Boonetown. This prior knowledge, coupled with what she had already inadvertently learned since her arrival was certainly providing her with quite a lot to consider. The snippets of conversation she was even then overhearing merely compounded her thoughts further. She concentrated again on the voices coming faintly through the heavy wood of the door. The second man in the room was murmuring something. Lizabeth could not distinguish anything he was saying, could not even identify his voice if she were to converse with him at some later time. The original speaker, however, much to her satisfaction, continued to speak in that loud, authoritative tone.

'Kill him if you have to, just get it done.' Lizabeth's head came up. Taggart was right, if she had a brain in her head she would never have followed him to Boonetown. She should get as far away as possible from Saul Jefferies and what he represented. There was more danger here than she had appreciated, and she finally began to understand why Taggart had felt justified in warning her off quite so strongly. And to think she had fancied herself attracted to Jefferies. She shuddered.

'Ma'am, what exactly are you doin'?' the bellhop asked, his face creased with suspicion and Lizabeth returned abruptly to the present and her current predicament. She stepped hastily away from the door, her face flushed guiltily. She could not have denied that she was eavesdropping. To have done so would merely draw further unwanted attention to her activities.

'My goodness, isn't that Mr Jefferies hurrying towards us?' she gasped, looking over the boy's shoulder. He turned but, of course, Jefferies was not to be seen, rather it was another gentleman, a stranger to Lizabeth who hurried upwards, taking the stairs two steps at a time.

In desperation she took the opportunity to unhook the small cameo brooch she had pinned earlier that morning to the high neck of her gown. She dropped it blindly, hearing it thud softly to the floor just as the gentleman, whom she now recognized as being another guest of the hotel, joined them.

'Ain't Mr Jefferies,' the bellhop said, stating the obvious, 'it's Mr Mills.'

'Good evenin', ma'am,' the latter acknowledged her, lifting his hat slightly. 'Miss FitzMaurice, ain't it?'

She inclined her head, a faintly puzzled expression on her face. 'I'm afraid you have the advantage, sir,' she was forced to admit.

'Mills, ma'am, Jonathan Mills. I heard Mr Jefferies give your name to the clerk below.'

Her face cleared. 'Mr Mills, how nice to meet you. You must certainly be of an observant nature.' She glanced around in rather an obvious fashion.

'You lose somethin', ma'am?' Mills obliged.

'Yes, I'm afraid so. I appear to have lost my brooch. It's rather a pretty thing, given to me by my mother.' They both began to search at this point. 'I'm not at all sure where, or even when, I could have lost it, which is rather stupid of me. I was trying to be discreet about my search. One feels such a fool, don't you agree, searching almost on hands and knees in a public place? I thought perhaps I might have dropped it along here as I came past. I'm almost sure I heard it fall. I was just about to enlist the help of the bellboy in my search when you came along.' She took pause to breathe at this point, glancing surreptitiously at the boy. He was obviously considering her position and hadn't quite made up his mind whether to believe her story or not.

'I'm not sure what he thought,' she laughed gaily, 'perhaps he imagined I was trying to eavesdrop or something.' She met the bellhop's eyes straight on and he had the grace to blush which reassured her immensely.

Jefferies' office door opened at this point and Lizabeth, for all her bravado, felt the blood rush from her face. Her palms began to sweat and a pulse leaped in her throat. She swallowed audibly. The two men emerging ended their conversation abruptly, eyeing Lizabeth and Mills with blatant suspicion.

'What on earth's goin' on here?' the smaller of the two demanded.

Mills straightened. 'Here it is, ma'am, musta rolled up along the wall when you dropped it.' He held the small cameo aloft in triumph, a satisfied beam on his pleasant face.

'Oh thank you so much, Mr Mills,' Lizabeth gushed, accepting the brooch. 'I'm so sorry if we disturbed you, gentlemen, but I lost my brooch and I was searching for it. Mr Mills was kind enough to offer his assistance.'

They continued to regard her in a disturbingly questioning manner for a long moment. 'How curious that you should have lost it in this precise spot,' the smaller man said softly, his eyes narrowed. She pretended not to notice anything amiss.

'Yes, wasn't it,' she agreed brightly. 'I was going to my room and heard it fall. I wasn't sure where it could have rolled to, but luckily Mr Mills found it. I suppose I was so nervous, that I didn't notice I had not fastened it securely.'

He raised an eyebrow. 'Nervous?' he queried.

'Why, of course. I do have an interview, in the morning I believe ... for the teaching position.'

'The interview, of course, I'd forgotten. You're the new schoolteacher Mr Jefferies advertised for.' He glanced at his companion who was impatiently hovering on the top step of the stairway. Apparently satisfied that she was patently harmless, he rejoined his companion and both descended to the hotel lobby.

Lizabeth knew she would remember the speaker in particular. There was something about him. Medium height, with a pleasant, nondescript face, he was obviously the more intelligent of the two and it was he who had been issuing orders within Jefferies' office. She wasn't absolutely sure he had believed her story, but it was the best she could come up with under the circumstances.

'My goodness,' she exclaimed, eyeing the second man, 'that gentleman looks like he could be a fist-fighter of some sort.' He was a squat individual with a large bulbous head and mean eyes.

She turned wide, questioning eyes to Jonathan Mills. He squared his shoulders, transparently pleased to be the subject of so much feminine attention. 'That there is Ben Jaeckell,' he replied. 'He works for Jefferies, kinda jack of all trades. He's a fighter all right, near killed Jim Taylor once.'

She pivoted. 'Taylor; isn't he one of the owners of the T.T. outfit?'

'The same. Jaeckell edged 'im on some. Taylor didn't have no choice.'

Lizabeth frowned. 'And Taylor, how did he fare?'

Mills rubbed the back of his neck. 'Now that's just it, we all thought he'd be killed for sure, 'specially when Jaeckell whacked 'im over the head with that bottle, but he managed to hold his own real good. Gave Jaeckell quite a hidin' if'n I recollect right. Wouldn't have lasted though, he was near spent when Tom Lawson took matters into his own hands.' He chuckled. 'Jaeckell spent five days in jail, didn't like it no way.

They had reached the second-storey landing by this time and Lizabeth slowly walked the long, empty hallway to her room at the end. Mills fell into step alongside her, the bellhop a few steps ahead.

'I've heard Mr Jefferies hopes to purchase the T.T. valley?' she said carefully.

Mills dug his hands into his pocket, fishing for his room key. 'Ma'am,' he replied fitting it into the lock, 'that's a matter of opinion round about.' He paused. 'Let me give you a little advice. You're a mighty pretty woman, too pretty to be botherin' your head 'bout things like T.T. and such like. Folks in town figure there's gonna be a range war. It might be for the best if'n you didn't ask them kinda questions, might not be healthy for you. Do you understand?'

She nodded. 'Thank you, Mr Mills,' she replied in a low voice, 'for finding my brooch and for ... everything.'

She paused at her own door, just two doors down from Mills' room. She smiled at the boy as he handed her her room key and tipped him much more than she could readily afford.

On entering the room she crossed to the dressing-table. Her face in the mirror above the table wore a pensive look, as she dropped the little cameo on to the table's smooth, polished surface.

NINE

'You gotta be jokin',' was Billy's amazed response to Tom Lawson's suggestion. 'Deputize me? I ain't no lawman, Tom.'

'Exactly.' Tom Lawson leaned forward eagerly. 'You could snoop round down there like no lawman could. One sniff the law was on to 'em, and I figure Jefferies'd call off them boys pronto. My sources tell me that Jefferies has been suspected of supplyin' the Indians with guns for sometime. I got me this gut feelin' he's involved all right, right up to his lily-livered neck. I know for a fact that liquor and gun-tradin' is operatin' round the fort area and Shorty Styles, one of Jefferies' right-hand men, has been spotted down that way more than once.'

He drew several times on his pipe, warming to the subject. 'I'd go myself, 'ceptin' them boys'd be sure to get pretty nervy if'n I was to suddenly show up. Could be months afore they'd surface again.'

Billy darted an uneasy glance at his companion. Outside in the street a wagon rumbled past, heading out of town. Once again there was the sound of boots passing on the sidewalk and, as before, both men waited for the sound to fade before resuming their conversation.

'Couldn't you call in a marshal,' Taggart suggested.

Lawson shrugged expressively. 'On hearsay?' he replied with dry sarcasm. 'On conjecture? Oh sure!'

Billy's thoughts were racing. He needed to

think some. He reclaimed his forgotten mug from the floor, pouring yet more coffee. Taking an exploratory mouthful, he grimaced.

'Needin' somethin',' Lawson grinned crookedly, passing the whiskey bottle. 'Better than honey any ole time.' This time Billy did not refuse the offer. He needed something stronger than coffee!

He was suddenly aware of exhaustion, a combination of days spent in the saddle, and a delayed reaction to the morning's events perhaps. He sat down wearily, the chair protesting loudly as it accepted his weight. He closed his eyes.

'I reckon you've a personal interest in takin' on this job,' Lawson pressed relentlessly.

'I have?' Taggart's eyes flew open and he raised one eyebrow, a rather ironic twist to his mouth. 'Can't think of one, not a one.'

Lawson grinned almost wickedly. 'Just consider,' he said, 'if Jefferies was lyin' in some stinkin' jail, he couldn't bother the T.T. none.' He paused for dramatic effect, sitting back, allowing the words to register. He took to smoking his pipe in quick, nervous draws. The blue smoke curled to the ceiling, the scent of the tobacco filled the room with its distinctive aroma.

'Jefferies is a mighty powerful man, make no mistake, Billy. If he's got a hankerin' for the T.T. valley, he might just take it.' Billy scowled. 'You'd best remember too, that some of them folk you care 'bout could maybe get 'emselves killed in the doin'.'

'Damn it, Tom, that's out and out blackmail,' Billy protested. He thought a moment. 'Why me, there's better qualified than me to take this on?'

'You know the country down there like the back of your hand and, more important, the folks in the fort know you as a horse breeder. They're used to seein' you come and go without raisin' any suspicions. Add that to the fact that you speak the lingo like a native and know the trails. Well, I'd say ain't nobody better qualified.' He looked Taggart straight in the eye. 'Besides,' he ended simply, 'ain't nobody I'd trust more.'

There was the beginning of an determined frown between Billy's eyes. The sheriff's pipe had long since extinguished itself, but he didn't notice clenching its stem tightly between his teeth. Foreseeing a categorical refusal, Lawson gathered his arguments for the final assault.

'Could maybe ask Jim, of course,' he began in a musing way. 'Him bein' a lawman one time I don't reckon he'd refuse. Still, some no-good might recognize 'em from way back. 'Course there's Jess to consider, her havin' no other family and all.'

Taggart lifted his head. 'You wouldn't,' he exclaimed helplessly.

'I want Jefferies,' Lawson replied in a hard way. 'I want him real bad. He's thinkin' of takin' over my town, and I won't have it.'

Billy suddenly laughed. 'Hell,' he muttered, 'you bring me to mind of an old hound dog on a scent. Hell bent on treein' me.'

It was almost dusk when Billy eventually left the jailhouse. He paused just for a moment within the shadows of the doorway. There was a tension still lingering in the gathering gloom, a kind of foreboding he could not pinpoint. He mentally straightened his shoulders as if against an imaginary onslaught.

He had managed, in the intervening hours, to snatch some sleep on a bunk in one of the vacant cells. In consequence, some of his earlier weariness had lifted. Figuring that Taylor would by now, have grown impatient he hurried, walking quickly towards the general store on Main Street. Finding it in darkness, he changed direction, heading instead for Clancy's Paradise, a small saloon off Main Street, and Taylor's favourite haunt when in town.

There were quite a number of the town's citizens strolling the sidewalk as it was still quite early in the evening. Billy could not but be acutely conscious of the speculative glances coming his way. One lady even crossed the street to avoid meeting him face to face.

The steady sound of sawing emitted from back of the town carpenter's place, and seemed to follow him relentlessly as he continued his journey. He did not have to turn his head to envisage the long, wooden box taking shape back there in the yard. Without checking, he knew that already, a newly turned mound of earth would be silhouetted as a grim reminder against the horizon up on Boothill. Pushing through the swing doors of Clancy's he welcomed the bright lights and frivolity as they wrapped round him like a blanket.

His opaque eyes flicked over the occupants of the smoky interior. Some he recognized as being on Jefferies' payroll. The spangled dresses of the dance-floor girls were brilliant whorls of colour in the drab surroundings. Blue smoke curled upwards and hovered, held captive by the low ceiling.

73

Clancy, the proprietor, stood in his habitual spot by the bar, watching the proceedings. He chewed thoughtfully on a fat cigar which he held to the side of his mouth. He struck a match deftly with his thumb nail and lit up, drawing deep on the well-bitten cigar. He expelled its thick smoke through his nose with obvious pleasure.

A big, burly Irish immigrant, trouble was nothing new to Jake Clancy. Seemed like he was born to trouble, had lived with its companionship all his life. He possessed the gift of knowing everything about everyone, without seeming in the least interested in anything. He had an accurate idea of how things were shaping up between Saul Jefferies and the T.T., but he wasn't about to voice an opinion aloud.

Billy covered the distance from the door to the bar in three long strides, calling for a glass. The young bartender threw Clancy an uncertain glance which did not go un-noticed by Billy. The big Irishman shook his head imperceptibly, indicating that he would serve the cowboy personally.

'Bad business earlier,' he commented carefully, watching Taggart throw off his drink. Billy grimaced as the raw liquor hit the back of his throat. Without acknowledging the other's remark, he refilled his glass, raising it in ironic salute, before its contents swiftly followed that of the first. 'Taylor been in?' he asked.

Clancy wiped the bar top absently. 'Yeah,' he replied. 'Was in earlier, told me if'n you showed up, to say he'd be back.' He folded the bar cloth in four, placing it neatly beneath the bar. 'You hungry, Taggart?' he queried suddenly in his pleasant, lilting accent.

'Reckon I am,' Billy said in surprise. 'Been near a day since I've eaten last. You got some of that stew of yours, I'd be much obliged.'

Like most Western saloonkeepers, Clancy kept a large pot of beef stew bubbling on the stove out back of the bar. Many a hungry traveller, down on his luck, had reason to be thankful for Clancy's grub, and that evening, Taggart was no exception.

While he ate, Rosa Lee James, the saloon's latest attraction, came on stage amid much cheering and cat-calling. In her low-cut dress, displaying a great deal of her charms, she presented a much appreciated diversion for the men present. She acknowledged the applause with a faint smile, launching without further encouragement into a slightly *risqué,* but highly amusing number. Judging from the noise which threatened to drown the piano accompaniment the majority of the drinkers knew, at the very least, a line or two from the chorus!

By the time Billy had cleared his third helping of the excellent stew, Rosa had come to the end of her long song. Under cover of the ensuing yells and floor stamping, Clancy leaned towards Billy to remark, 'Taylor's back, got that Lucky Hale with him.' He leaned a little closer. 'Don't want no trouble in my saloon, if'n it can be avoided, you hear?'

Taggart grinned, his eyes crinkled up a little at the corners. ''Course, if it can't be avoided, now that's different ain't it?'

'Ain't it just,' Clancy agreed rather gleefully. Taylor accepted a glass of beer, nodding his thanks to Clancy. Billy was aware of a tension in his partner. He raised a questioning eyebrow, but said nothing.

'We got us some new trouble, I reckon,' Taylor burst out, having drained his beer. 'That damn Jefferies gave out orders that nobody, if'n they know what's good for 'em, is to help us. Wouldn't serve us at the store, nothin'.'

The two men exchanged a look. 'Damn,' Billy bit out.

TEN

'What you need right now is a plan.' Lucky broke the silence which followed Taylor's blunt announcement. His two companions turned to regard him questioningly. 'You got a plan how we're gonna get us enough provisions to last until Jefferies comes to his senses?' Taylor said, in an impatient voice. Lucky studiously avoided meeting his eyes. He nodded with contrived nonchalance towards Clancy who, correctly interpreting the gesture pushed a glass of beer along the full length of the bar top.

Lucky caught the foam-topped glass deftly. He took his time emptying almost half its contents before continuing. 'I reckon if'n there was some kinda diversion like, say, a fight here in the Paradise, you boys could load up that buckboard and high-tail it out of town afore anyone was the wiser.' He drained his beer and twisted the empty glass in his hands. 'Don't you think?'

He was inexplicably keyed up and it showed. 'Listen,' he plunged on, oddly intense, 'I'd sure feel better about livin' out on the ranch if'n you was to let me try out what I've got in mind.' Taylor frowned and shook his head.

'Pa'd want it too if'n he was here right now,' he grinned suddenly, 'which he ain't. Hell, I've been in scrapes afore, ain't got killed yet.' He paused to draw breath. 'You just be sure you pay for them supplies. Don't want to be thrown into jail for no stealin'. Pa'd kill me himself for that.'

His companions were still not totally convinced, but Lucky could see them weaken some. 'Ain't a kid no more,' he plunged on, 'gotta do what I think is right, don't I?'

Taggart shrugged. 'Reckon you do at that, but don't seem right lettin' you take a damn fool risk like this.'

Lucky scowled. 'Ain't your decision,' he bit out.

Taggart exchanged a private glance with Taylor. 'Looks like he's made up his mind, don't it?'

The latter nodded. 'Just don't do nothin' out 'n' out foolish, you hear? If n you was to get hurt bad your pa'd probably have our hides for boot laces.' Both drained their glasses and called for a refill.

'Best get goin' then,' Taggart muttered a

little later, 'got us a busy night ahead.'

As they threaded their way through the tables scattered about the saloon, they encountered Ben Jaeckell making his way into the Paradise. They exchanged no words, but Jaeckell paused long enough to throw a black look in their general direction. Lucky took to watching Jaeckell in the mirror which hung over the bar. He did not like Jaeckell. He did not trust him. His raw brutality repulsed him.

Now that he had finally succeeded in having his way Lucky felt strangely bereft and more than a little on edge. He called for another beer and mentally counted the minutes as they passed. How long did it take three men to hitch up a buckboard and make their way to the general store? He couldn't be sure! Jaeckell meanwhile was leaning backwards against the bar mere inches from Lucky.

'Howdy, Hale,' he called. There was something mocking in the words. 'Didn't expect to see you in town for a spell yet,' he continued. He guffawed. Someone back of the saloon sniggered.

'Free country, ain't it.' Lucky swirled a mouthful of beer round his teeth. 'Can come into town if'n I've a mind.'

Jaeckell glanced round for the benefit of his supporters. 'Just figured you'd be ashamed to show your face. Any man worth his salt would, bein' that you're livin' on charity and all.' Before Lucky could reply Jaeckell bellowed down the bar, 'A glass up here, Clancy. Me and my friend are gonna have us a little ole drink.'

Lucky straightened to his full height. He eyed the other man full on. 'Got my own, thanks,' he said in conversational tones. 'Besides,' he added, 'don't drink with scum like you.' With that an uneasy silence prevailed speckled by a tension that throbbed and twisted.

Jaeckell pushed the bottle closer to his younger companion. 'Drink,' he ordered in an ugly voice.

Lucky met Jaeckell's eyes in the mirror. 'You heard me first time,' he said, in that same pleasant conversational way, 'don't want no drink from you.'

Jaeckell's face was fast changing colour. 'You tryin' to insult me, boy?' he bellowed.

Lucky smiled caustically. 'Take it whatever way you've a mind,' he said, his voice alive with a careless devilry. Jaeckell lunged for his gun. There was a stir as the watchers drew back expectantly. 'You so much as touch that gunbelt,' Lucky muttered in a quiet voice, 'and I'll kill you where you stand.' He did not turn as he spoke. There was no change of intonation in his voice just a flat sureness which Jaeckell could not mistake. As it happened Jaeckell much preferred to fight with his fists or with his knife.

'Suits me just fine,' he said now with relish and dropped his gunbelt.

'Reckon this has gone just about far enough,' Clancy spoke with authority. His voice cut through the atmosphere like a hunting knife through fresh meat. 'Don't want no bloodshed in my saloon.' He held a sawn-off shot-gun in his big hands. 'Ain't takin' sides mind, but I reckon four 'gainst one ain't fair odds.' He eyed Jaeckell's companions and then Jaeckell. 'Always did take you for a yellow-bellied coward,' he remarked.

'Best take care, Clancy,' Jaeckell retorted. 'I don't forget easy.'

Clancy grinned roguishly. 'Better men than you'll ever be have tried, me boyo. But as you see, I'm still here.' He gestured with the shot-gun. 'Lucky, you move along now. Find that horse of yours and get. I'll hold these vermin for a spell, give you a head start. After that you're on your own though.'

Lucky threw a quick look towards the swing doors. 'Can't do that, Clancy,' he muttered through his teeth, 'gotta finish this.'

Clancy followed the cowboy's eyes as they swung to the door. He caught a quick glimpse of the T.T. buckboard as it headed down a side street. It was soon swallowed up in the darkness. 'Damnation,' he muttered under his breath as the true situation became clear.

'You want blood' – Lucky too had dropped his gunbelt – 'come and get it.' He stepped away from the bar. 'What's the matter,' he jeered, 'scared I'll bust you wide open?'

Jaeckell's initial surprise quickly became pleasure. He flexed his muscles some and his supporters cheered.

'You remind me of a fool rooster we've got out on the T.T., always fluffin' himself up for the benefit of the hen coop,' Lucky laughed. He pivoted suddenly and caught Jaeckell just under the chin with the full force of his closed fist. The big man staggered. His teeth dug into his lip and blood spouted from the cut. He ran his tongue over the wound tasting the blood like some crazed animal.

In the general confusion some of his men

again edged forward. Clancy swung the shot-gun in a wide arc. 'This here fight,' he bellowed, 'is between them two. Don't need no help.'

Tough as old rawhide, Jaeckell pulled himself erect with ease. An unpleasant grimace which might have been mistaken for a grin split his mashed lips. He moved with more speed than his bulk had led Lucky to believe. He took his first blow just below the rib cage. It felt as if a mule had kicked him. Lucky fell back, desperately trying to protect his face from the ensuing onslaught. He was gasping for breath and held Jaeckell at bay with increasing difficulty.

Perceiving that he had the advantage Jaeckell was quick to capitalize. He moved in swiftly, lowering his massive head and charged. Lucky side-stepped at the last moment. He heard the table behind him splinter clean in half as it took the full impact of Jaeckell's fall. He stood back and made the most of the brief reprieve while the other man regained his feet.

Jaeckell's face was a mess of blood and bruises. His expression had become increasingly brutal, sort of wild. Scrabbling to his feet he re-entered the fray with renewed ferocity. Although bigger and certainly stronger than his younger opponent, Jaeckell did not possess Lucky's fleetness of foot or his natural skill. Both men, however, were beginning to show physical signs of the continuing battle. Their clothes were torn and splattered with blood. Lucky suspected that just maybe he had busted his hand in the first encounter. Damn, son of a bitch, it was like hitting a solid stone wall! Still, there was the dubious satisfaction of having slipped in some telling jabs past the big man's guard.

It was obvious, even to a casual observer that Lucky was tiring. The cowboy couldn't take much more of that kind of battering. Jaeckell's last punch had caught him on the side of the head. It knocked him off balance and Jaeckell bent to follow through with a kick to the guts. Lucky just about managed to roll clear, escaping serious injury by a mere hair's breadth. Completing his roll he made it to his knees before Jaeckell had fully recovered from his surprise.

Lucky shook his head. There was a singing in his ears and his head hurt right to his boots. He didn't feel so good, but managed to rally sufficiently to fend off Jaeckell's next assault.

The big man came in like a raging bull. He

swung his booted foot intending it for Lucky's face. Kneeling as he was, Lucky could only reach upwards and grab the other's boot in his hands. He pushed with all his remaining strength. Jaeckell fell badly, the impact shaking him to the core. He lay there for some time in an unwieldy heap, gasping loudly. Blood ran in a slow trickle from his nose. Studying him, Lucky was fairly sure he had broken it.

He leaned unsteadily against a nearby table. It shifted beneath him and he hadn't the energy to counteract it. He fell anew to the sawdust. The dirt mingled with the blood in his mouth.

Hell, how had it come to this? The past week's events had torn his life to shreds, had devastated the lives of his family and friends, and for what? With the rapid ebb of physical resilience a wave of depression, totally at odds with his spirit, gradually washed over him.

'Damn you to hell,' he whispered fiercely. He dragged himself upright by sheer will-power and glared impotently at Jaeckell.

ELEVEN

Clancy watched without real interest, as the fight progressed. Wasn't his fight! Still, the kid was taking some beating, maybe it was time to put a stop to it.

'OK, Jaeckell,' he called, 'reckon he's taken enough punishment.' Jaeckell appeared not to hear. He watched as Lucky circled the upturned table, swaying a little.

'Ain't over yet,' he said, spitting blood, 'not 'till I say so.'

Lucky was having trouble focusing. How far had the buckboard gone? he wondered. Gotta have those supplies; must keep going; promised! Promised! Gave his word!

Jaeckell kept on coming, anticipation of a kill gleaming savagely in those animal eyes. Lucky could do little except wait like some helpless sacrifice. He was physically unable to repulse the onslaught and prepared to defend himself as best he could under the circumstances. It was all he could do.

Taggart's entrance on the scene came as a dreadful anticlimax. The whole impulse of the gathering fell flat. Those who, only moments before had been baying for blood, were now curiously silent and uneasy.

There was an ambience of barely controlled fury about Taggart, an aura of indomitability that was almost palpable. Most of those present knew Taggart but they had never seen him quite this way. In that moment, and in that mood, they feared him.

Sensing the change at last Jaeckell spun round. He had the look of a hungry wolf defending a kill. 'This here ain't your fight, Taggart,' he growled. Taggart continued to stand on the threshold, a dark, menacing shadow against the outer darkness of the night. His cold eyes raked round the gathering as he stepped into the light. 'Ain't your damn fight,' Jaeckell repeated. 'Butt out.'

Taggart's teeth gleamed white in his brown face. 'Is now,' he said, stepping forward. His arm swung in a wide arc, his fist making contact with Jaeckell just on the point of his chin. The big man fell backwards out cold before he hit the Paradise's dirt floor.

The crowd shuffled back a pace or two. One fool, in a burst of misguided loyalty, went for his gun. Taggart caught the slight movement from the corner of his eye. He drew his own weapon, swift and smooth and deadly. There was no mercy in him then, only a red-hot anger which threatened to burn him up. The man stumbled to the ground, a big red stain spreading rapidly across his shirt front. No one moved, hardly dared to breathe.

Taggart's eyes continued to rake them, daring someone to do something, anything, so that he could unleash the full beast of his anger. 'Get out of my sight,' he snapped, as no one obliged. He nudged Jaeckell's inert bulk with the toe of his boot, a look of acute distaste on his thin face. 'And take him with you. Reckon the show's over, folks,' he continued in cold tones. 'Sure hope you all got your money's worth.'

He lunged quickly, just in time to catch Lucky as the latter pitched forward. 'Ain't you supposed to be on your way back to the ranch?' he mumbled through mashed lips, steadying himself with Taggart's help.

'Came back for you,' Taggart replied shortly, some of the anger remaining, 'you damn fool. Wasn't there nobody 'ceptin' Jaeckell you could pick a fight with?'

Lucky pushed him away. 'Don't knock me down with gratitude or nothin',' he grumbled crossly, 'and quit your damn fussin'', I'm fine.' He grabbed at a half-empty bottle of whiskey and took a long draught, grimacing as the raw liquor hit his stomach.

He leaned backwards against the bar top, steadying himself and explored his face, wiping some of the blood away. He took another swig of the whiskey, swirling it round his teeth, moaning a little beneath his breath. 'Hell, what took you so long?' he quipped suddenly, sounding more like himself. 'Beginnin' to think you was never gonna show.' He spoke with a kind of wryness though, that made the mobile mouth look uncharacteristically wary, just a little sour. Billy bent forward and picked up Lucky's hat where it lay in the sawdust. He dusted it off thoughtfully, before ramming it none too gently on to his companion's head.

'Come on,' he said, 'lets see 'bout gettin' you back to the ranch.' He grunted, hitching an arm round Lucky's waist, taking his full weight.

'I don't feel too good,' the latter stated the obvious with an apologetic shrug. 'Ain't sure I could sit a horse. Sure can't ride the sorrel.' He ran a bloodied hand across his face, wincing. 'Next time I get me a noble notion I want your promise that you'll kick the seat of my pants 'till I see sense, you hear?'

'Still,' Billy said, relenting a little, 'your idea worked out real good. Half the town came down to the saloon to see what all the excitement was 'bout. The buckboard must be near half-way to the ranch by now.' The faintest whisper of silk caused him to break off the conversation abruptly and turn. 'Ma'am?' he said.

'You don't need to travel back tonight,' Rosa Lee said softly, making no secret of having heard at least part of their conversation. Her slim hand came up, detaining Billy. 'At least let me clean him up some,' she continued. Taggart hesitated, anxious to be on his way. 'He'll slow you down, way he is now.'

Lucky slumped a little, his head coming forward on to his chest. Taggart frowned. 'Maybe you've got a point,' he agreed. 'Was considerin' tyin' 'im to his saddle, but reckon he's taken enough for one night. Besides, I got me an errand to run afore I leave. You take care of him, ma'am, and much obliged. I'll be along later.'

He stalked away, giving Lucky little opportunity to argue. 'Hi, where you goin'?' he did manage to yell. Taggart stopped,

90

tipped his hat forward over his eyes, but did not turn. Head lowered on to his chest, he said, 'Gotta go see Tom Lawson 'bout somethin' we discussed earlier. Be ready to move afore first light, come mornin', 'cos I ain't waitin'.'

Taggart was as angry as he had ever recalled being. It went deep to the very essence of him, that those things he held most dear should be so ransomed by a man of Jefferies' calibre. The very thought soiled what was, until then, something untouchable. It violated the very sanctity of his home and that could not, and would not, be endorsed by any part of him. He had not fully acknowledged until he had walked into that saloon the extent of his anger. When he saw those blood-thirsty fools applaud carnage as being equivalent to the best the town had to offer in entertainment, he truly appreciated the courage exhibited by the young cowboy at centre stage.

In that instant, he had seemed to Taggart to be the most unlikely but, nevertheless, the finest of heroes. The contrast between honour and dishonour in that moment was so great that it remained indelibly engraved on his mind and was to serve in the weeks ahead as an infinite source of fuel for his anger. He lowered his head like a young bull preparing to defend his supremacy. If Jefferies took the T.T. then he vowed it would be only at great cost. He wondered just how high a price Jefferies was willing to pay, or if indeed he had even considered the cost at all.

TWELVE

'I trust the evening's entertainment hasn't fatigued you too unduly, Miss FitzMaurice? The town council and the more influential ladies were anxious to meet you as soon as you arrived.'

Lizabeth glanced at the man by her side. She smiled with genuine pleasure. The gesture lit her face to unexpected beauty, crinkling the almond-shaped grey eyes to beguiling gaiety. 'No indeed, Mr Jefferies,' she responded, her voice light and carefree. 'I have enjoyed the entire evening immensely. It was most kind of the committee to take the trouble to welcome me to Boonetown.'

Unexpectedly, Lizabeth found she had

indeed enjoyed the evening, much more than she had earlier anticipated. Alone in her room with nothing but the torrent of her thoughts she could not have envisioned participating in the proposed event with any real enthusiasm. She had been exhausted then, and in dire need of a bath. Her spirits had dipped to rock bottom and she had found herself longing for her friends and for the familiar surroundings of the fort. She had cried a little before finally falling into a deep and surprisingly dreamless sleep, completely worn out.

On waking some hours later, she had stretched, propped herself up on the goose-down pillows and studied her surroundings with a less jaundiced eye. She ran her hand softly across the fine woollen bed cover and sighed, her spirits lifting. She yawned, eyeing the sunny yellow curtains and the contrasting grey of the tastefully chosen wall colour. She had never seen a more beautiful room, and certainly not during the previous ten days' stage trip.

There had been stop-overs, of course, to change teams, and while they had been a welcome reprieve from the continuous travelling, Lizabeth remembered one particular straw mattress which had persistently rustled, even when she had lain perfectly still. Her slumber in this obviously clean and tasteful room in contrast had refreshed and revitalized her, as had the warm and scented bath in which she had wallowed upon waking.

During the course of the evening's entertainment, Jefferies had proved himself a witty and charming escort, forcing her yet again to review her earlier assessment of his character. His manner was attentive and gentlemanlike. If, now and then, she suspected a hidden motive behind his more abstruse comments, she chose to overlook it on that particular occasion.

'What a lovely night,' she said, looking upwards to the inky heavens. The stars twinkled brilliantly like a glorious diamond necklace nesting against the velvet night sky. She picked out the Little Bear with ease. Judging from the position of the North Star, she figured it to be about eleven o'clock, perhaps a little later.

Jefferies didn't immediately reply. Perhaps, Lizabeth thought, there was nothing he could say. She searched her mind for other avenues of small talk when she sensed rather than saw her companion stiffen. He lost a step, faltered, but catching her watching him he quickly recollected himself.

'Evenin',' a voice she instantly recognized caused Lizabeth to spin round, her hand going involuntarily to her mouth. Her eyes held Taggart's for a brief heart-stopping moment, and she could not quite hide the gladness she felt at finally seeing him face to face. Lizabeth was mistaken in her assumption that Taggart had not seen her earlier. He had indeed spotted her among those gathered and the sense of shock he had experienced still lingered. Some emotion she could not identify flickered strangely across his face and a small pulse throbbed with the beat of his heart just behind his jawline. Otherwise he betrayed no sign of what he might be thinking, encountering her here in Boonetown of all places and with Saul Jefferies of all people, when he had thought her still at the fort.

'You know each other?' It was a statement not a question. Jefferies glanced into each face in turn, managing to keep his own council with considerable effort. He hadn't mistaken the tension between them, and mixed with curiosity there was a sense of suspicion and an unexpected anger.

Taggart shrugged in a careless manner. 'Kinda,' he replied, 'I'm acquainted with the folks at the fort who gave Lizabeth a roof.'

Jefferies arched an eyebrow. 'Indeed,' he said and there was profound irony in the tone.

'The Washingtons,' Lizabeth inserted quickly. 'You recall me mentioning them.'

'Indeed.'

Taggart's glance shifted from Lizabeth. 'I hear you're interested in buyin' our ranch,' he said, abruptly changing the subject.

'I assume you've spoken with Taylor,' Jefferies replied, watching Taggart, his face bland and urbane. Lizabeth frowned, sensing the challenge inherent in the tone both men employed during the interchange. There was rather an uncomfortable pause.

Taggart shifted his weight a little. 'Indeed,' he said, in subtle imitation of Jefferies' earlier response.

'I made him a fair offer.' Jefferies flung back his head, lifting his chin in an aggressive manner.

'And we refused,' Taggart replied, in a soft and dangerous voice.

Lizabeth risked a quick look at Jefferies, feeling the hot colour stain her cheeks, but managing in a false, overly bright voice to comment on how late it was, and how small the world was, and how nice it was to meet old friends. Both men ignored her.

'It's later than I realized,' she continued, with determination, 'and it's been a long day. If you gentlemen will excuse me I think I shall retire.' She nodded coolly in their general direction and continued alone into the hotel. She was not insensible to the tension which had immediately been obvious between the two protagonists she was leaving. She climbed the entrance stairs quickly and paused at the top to catch her breath.

'You thought some more on my offer?' Jefferies' voice floated up from below her. She glanced carefully over the handrail, shamelessly eavesdropping. It was becoming a habit, she observed with a whimsical smile.

'I thought it over,' Taggart replied, in a deliberately provoking way, 'for all of two seconds. Ain't sellin'.'

'We'll see...'

Taggart's hands clenched to fists, the bid for control showing briefly on the chiselled face. 'Ain't the time, Jefferies,' he muttered, in a voice so low she was forced to lean forward to hear. 'Soon though, real soon, you gonna wish you never set eyes on the T.T. valley, by Gawd, you will.'

He glanced upwards then, his expression brutal in its raw anger. Lizabeth had been mistaken in her assumption that he wasn't aware of her listening. Their eyes clashed yet again and she stepped back a little. Something chilled inside her as she watched him walk away into the night.

THIRTEEN

Taggart's meeting with Tom Lawson had left him feeling disgruntled to put it mildly and his surprise encounter with Lizabeth had done little to improve that evening's foul temper. However, his talk with Lawson had to some extent defused the awful sense of helplessness he had been feeling. His step on leaving the jailhouse had held a new determination. If Saul Jefferies had been able to read the thoughts circling Taggart's head at that moment he would most certainly have slept less easy in his big, custom-made bed. There were dark, brooding places inside Taggart which were relentless when stirred to life. In that respect he was rather like a hungry mountain lion, once he sank his teeth into a prey, it was mighty difficult to prise him loose. The boy who had come to kill him had seen something of that darkness and even he, who had not understood at all, had recognized the danger.

There was something of that uncompromising tenacity evident in his eyes as he paused to stare upwards at Jefferies' hotel. He fished in his vest pocket for the makings and rolled the loose tobacco round the ball of his hand in a slow, pensive movement. His eyes narrowed. Perhaps one of those windows, still lighted despite the hour, was Lizabeth's. He scowled, crushing the unlit cigarette in a savage manner between his fingers.

He'd a good mind to find her room right there and then and give her a piece of his mind. The little fool; he'd told her not to come. When he got his hands on her he'd paddle her butt so hard she wouldn't sit comfortably for a month. Then, he bared his teeth in escalating fury, he'd put her on the first stage back to the fort.

He flicked the mangled remains of the cigarette to the ground impatiently and began to roll a second. This one he completed and, taking a long, steadying draft of the smoke, he felt somewhat calmer. He stepped back into the deeper shadows cast by the balcony above and dipped his head a little, his face heavy in thought. Only the red glow of his cigarette tip indicated his presence. Having finished his smoke he extinguished the butt with the toe of a worn boot, but did not leave. He remained motionless for a long time in the shadows, his expression flinty beneath the rim of his stetson.

The night was cool and very still. A coyote howled somewhere in the hills beyond the town. Taggart imagined that he could catch the scent of pines in the air and his longing for morning was suddenly very strong, his sense of foreboding hourly more urgent.

Finally, as if coming to a decision, he left the relative safety of his hiding-place. He blew on his hands for a moment, flexing the fingers. His feet had long since frozen and he stamped them in a futile attempt at warming them. With movement came returning sensation and he gritted his teeth against the pins and needles, cursing himself for all kinds of a fool.

The lobby was deserted except for the night clerk, who at that hour was sound asleep in his chair behind the hotel desk. Taggart carefully leafed through the guest book until he found Lizabeth's distinctive scrawl. Her room number was conveniently indicated beside her signature. He found her room without incident.

'Liz,' he whispered into the wood, tapping as hard as he dared on her door. 'Lizabeth,' he repeated with growing exasperation, 'it's me, open this damn door.' He pressed his ear against the wood but heard nothing. 'Lizabeth,' he tried again, this time with growing impatience. 'I gotta talk to you; come on, Liz, open the door.' He paused, holding his breath, but nothing happened. 'Don't be stubborn, let me in, you hear me.' He rapped the door with more force than he had intended. He glanced round anxiously, but all the other hotel occupants appeared to be sleeping soundly. He let out his breath on a sigh, not aware then that he had been holding it.

'Liz, you open this door this instant, or I swear I'll kick the damn thing down.' He heard her fumbling with the bolt, and then a pause as if she was reconsidering. 'Liz,' he hissed in a furious voice. The door opened.

'Hello, Taggart,' Lizabeth said in a tentative way. She stepped aside to allow him entrance. After the merest hesitation and a quick glance up and down the hallway, he slipped inside, closing the door silently behind him.

Once inside his eyes assessed the room.

Already she had made it her own. Her belongings were scattered in organized chaos over every available surface. His frown deepened as he noticed her evening cloak flung in a careless fashion across the soft, woollen bedcover together with the little matching beaded evening bag she liked so much.

'What in tarnation are you doin' here?' he demanded suddenly, unconsciously beginning to pace the room. He sniffed catching a faint whiff of the delicate perfume she wore. Somehow it merely increased the restlessness inside him. He ran his fingertips across the furniture, through the silky fabric of her evening cloak, over the leather of her books, finally coming to rest on the gilt-edged invitation card which had come by personal delivery from the town council earlier that same evening.

Lizabeth watched him in that considering way of hers. 'For the moment I live here,' she replied, being deliberately obtuse. 'This is my room.'

He stopped his pacing abruptly, his mouth tightened. 'Damn it, you know what I mean, what the hell are you doin' here in Boonetown, at this time of all times, just when it's brewin' up to a range war?'

She eyed him steadily. 'Not that it's any of your business, Mr Taggart,' she said in a cool voice, 'but I came here in reply to an advertisement for a schoolteacher.' Her tone seemed almost to dare him to suggest that there was any other motive behind her arrival, and her eyes were as flinty as his when she looked at him.

'But Boonetown...' he muttered inadequately.

'And why not Boonetown?' she retorted, nettled. 'Doesn't Boonetown need schooling like any other place, or is it too progressive?'

He rubbed his hand back and forth across his chin in a thoughtful way, his forehead furrowed. It crossed his mind that perhaps Lizabeth didn't see the situation in quite the same light as he, and that kinda stopped him in his tracks. He found himself disconcertingly inadequate in trying to fathom his next move, and so he blundered on.

'Well, you ain't stayin' here,' he practically yelled. 'I'm headin' out to the ranch first thing in the mornin' and I'm takin' you along. It'll be safer for you out on the T.T.' She flung back her head in the way he had come to know too well, and he realized with dismay that he had handled her wrongly.

Lizabeth was like Lucky's damn sorrel, needed coaxin'.

'What,' she practically spat, 'gives you the right to come into my room at an hour, I might add, when no real gentleman would come to a lady's room, and order me around as if I was one of the hands out on your precious ranch? I don't need your permission to remain here, nor do I need your permission to accept or decline Mr Jefferies' offer.' She took a deep breath. 'Do I make myself clear?' she added in glacial tones.

'Perfectly clear.'

She eyed him uncertainly as he resumed his pacing. For some moments there was silence in the room. 'Now let me make somethin' real clear,' he said in a quiet voice, the very softness of his words catching her attention as his previous anger had not. 'It's damn dangerous for you here in town right now. Jefferies knows that ... well, that we're close friends. He saw us tonight and he ain't no fool. That puts you in a dangerous spot and for your sake, if not because I want you to, you gotta do like I say and come to the ranch. Do I make myself clear?'

'Perfectly clear.'

If he had not been so preoccupied with

other matters, he might have been more suspicious of her sudden docility. As it was he was merely grateful that she accepted what he said so meekly. 'I brought you these, they're a mite big I know, but there'll be some ridin' tomorrow and it'll be easier if you're wearin' pants.' She caught the man's pants and shirt as he flung them in her general direction and held them up for inspection. The pants were obviously far too large. 'You gotta belt?' he muttered, between laughter and embarrassment as she pivoted for his approval.

Suddenly she looked up and unleashed her smile. It lit her face to that unexpected beauty which had so captivated Jefferies earlier that same evening. Billy held his breath, and found himself caught in her spell of gaiety and brightness. He reached out as if he couldn't help himself and touched her cheek very softly. Her skin was silky, smooth and warm. Her smile faded and something else, a dreamy quality animated her features to a beauty that was all sensation and nothing of gaiety. She turned her face into his hand and closed her eyes. It was as if she had crept into him, touched him inside his head, and the feeling she evoked was like whiskey on an empty stomach.

FOURTEEN

'You'll come then.' He managed to drag himself back to the present with considerable effort. His voice, even to his own ears was thick and hoarse.

'Come?' She opened her eyes slowly. 'Of course.' He smiled his relief. 'But not tonight, I'll meet you by the livery stable in the morning. I want to sleep in my comfortable bed in this beautiful room for just one night at least.'

'Damn it, Liz,' he began, 'that ain't what I had in mind. You must...'

A soft rap on the door interrupted whatever Taggart had meant to say. He laid his hand gently across her lips as Lizabeth turned towards him. Her eyes were wide and a little afraid.

'Miss FitzMaurice,' Jefferies' voice called in a low tone from the hallway, 'may I speak with you?'

Taggart nodded. He moved with care to hug the wall behind the door. Lizabeth looked towards him for guidance. He

106

nodded a second time, pointing towards the door. She drew an audible breath, straightened her hair nervously and opened the door a mere crack. 'It's rather late, Mr Jefferies,' she said. 'Could this not wait until the morning when I'm more refreshed? It's been rather a long day and I fear it's beginning to tell now.'

He noted her heightened colour and the brightness of her eyes without comment, but made a mental note of the fact nevertheless.

'I thought you might like to join me in a nightcap,' he said in a persuasive way. 'I wouldn't detain you too long, I promise.' He pushed forward almost imperceptibly as he spoke, his eyes searching the room over her shoulder. Taggart held his breath, his hand dropping to his gun.

Lizabeth had not failed to notice the quality of Jefferies' glance into the room and her anxiety for Taggart's safety zoomed upwards in a heart-stopping way. Dredging up her most spectacular smile, she positively dazzled Jefferies so that he, at least momentarily, forgot his suspicions.

'Perhaps just a little nightcap would be nice,' she acquiesced. 'I'll just get my shawl. Shouldn't be a moment.' She closed the door with a gentle click, and turning towards the bed, grabbed the shawl. Taggart dogged her footsteps all the way.

'What the hell do you think you're doin'?' he demanded, in a fierce whisper.

'Giving you the opportunity to escape as fast as you can. What do you think will happen if Jefferies finds you here? Don't be so damn stubborn, Taggart, do like I ask, just this once.'

He frowned, remembering Jefferies predatory look earlier. 'What if...' he began.

'Hush,' Lizabeth whispered and kissed him, a quick, fleeting touch of lips. 'What did I say about no true gentleman coming to a lady's room at this late hour?' she whispered into his ear. He grinned despite himself. 'Not sure whether that means you and Jefferies aren't gentlemen, or that I'm no lady.' She dipped her head to one side in a considering way. 'Meet you at first light,' she grinned impishly. 'Don't be late, you hear?' With that final quip, she swept across the room and out to join Jefferies He heard their voices fade to a distant murmur, and the sound of Lizabeth's tinkling laugh.

He figured it was maybe half past one, perhaps a mite later, when he left the hotel by the back entrance. His earlier foul mood had returned and he was mean and dangerous as a wolf. He figured he might as well head for the livery stable, try to get some shut-eye. He glanced upwards, eyeing the sky. It would be a long night.

He wasn't sure when he first became aware of being followed, but suddenly the smell of danger was strong in the night. His hand dropped to his gun holster and he curled his fingers round the familiar curve of the Colt which nestled there. His eyes flickered quickly from side to side as he sought to catch any faint movement in his peripheral vision. He slowed his pace a little, straining to catch any sound. There was nothing to indicate that he was in danger, but every fibre of him knew that there was someone out there, somewhere in the darkness.

Taking a deep breath, he steadied himself and without warning he sprinted forward, his long legs covering the distance with ease. He entered the interior of the livery stable at a fast gallop, displaying more urgency than grace. A shot whined over his head and embedded itself in the wooden doorway as he ducked inside. He fancied he had felt the heat of its passing.

Once inside, he blinked to adjust his eyes

to the new gloom. The horses stabled within stirred, unsettled by the shot and, in the confusion, Taggart disappeared somewhere among the sacks of grain and the saddles slung over the saddle rails. He crouched low, the smell of leather and horse and grain all around him, engulfing him in a strangely comforting way. He waited and the darkness inside him erupted in awful fury.

For a time nothing happened. Either the townsfolk had not heard the shot, or chose not to become involved. The horses settled down again, and only the odd rustling of straw broke the silence. Above in the loft, Taggart could hear some small night creature scratch about, and away in the hills that same coyote cried to the moon.

Taggart found himself clenching his jaw and he relaxed with effort. He edged forward a little and peered around the grain sacks. A shadow, long and growing was etched like a cardboard cut-out on the livery's dirt floor. As Taggart continued to watch, the barrel of a rifle, followed cautiously by its owner, edged slowly round the door-frame. Starlight glinted dully on the metal, while at the same time it elongated the shadow on the floor.

'Come on,' Taggart whispered fiercely,

'come and get what's comin'.'

He fired then and, as before, there was no mercy in him. His assailant fell with a heavy thud to the ground and Taggart's teeth gleamed briefly in the gloom. In almost the same instant he heard a spur rattle softly on stone. The sound came from the back of the building. Taggart spun, dropping to one knee and firing blindly at the sound. He heard the bullet hit home and a man grunted in pain. In the same movement Taggart had rolled on to his belly, aiming low in the general direction of the front entrance. The doorway was now completely empty, only pale light streaming through, the long, thin shadow of the rifle viciously swept away.

Taggart heard running feet and the sound of many voices. 'Heard shootin',' someone yelled, 'over yonder by the livery.' Taggart plunged silently towards the back of the stable, swinging himself upwards into the loft. He quickly crawled across the straw, just managing to reach the loft's outer door as the first of the townsfolk entered the stable below. Someone called for a lantern and Taggart recognized Tom Lawson's voice. By then he had swung himself down to the ground and quietly vanished.

Much later, when all had quietened down he returned to the livery and saddled up three horses, his own grey gelding among them. He led them to shelter in the willow grove off the back of the livery and settled down to wait for first light. He had been right in one respect, it was a long night.

FIFTEEN

Having joined Jefferies for the nightcap, Lizabeth had pleaded a headache, brought on she explained by the excitement of her day, and made a hasty retreat. But when she finally reached her room she found she could not stop the racing of her thoughts.

She had of course imagined her meeting with Billy many times during her journey to Boonetown. However, even her vivid, and it was vivid, imagination had not prepared her for the tension and the pleasure of that meeting. She touched her cheek where his fingers had caressed her and her heart raced. She paced the room, touching the furniture as she passed in much the same manner as Taggart had done earlier, restless

112

as a trapped wild animal.

The room was no longer sunny and cheerful, it had become a cage. Finally, unable to stand being indoors, she had retraced her steps, slipping from the hotel out into the night air. She had walked for a time, unwisely given the hour, but too unsettled to care. Her thoughts were in turmoil, churning futilely inside her head. The plan had formed even while Taggart had been warning her of the danger of her position, and the more she considered the better it had seemed to her. Needless to say it had much to do with her docile acceptance of Taggart's forceful suggestion that she should leave with him for the ranch.

While she did intend to keep her promise to meet him at first light, she had things to do in the interim which she knew would anger him greatly. But still, she smiled with satisfaction, when it proved successful, as of course it would, then he would be too pleased with her to be angry.

Finally deciding to return to the hotel, she had found it in almost total darkness. She estimated it to be about two o'clock in the morning and she figured that all the occupants would by now be asleep. She crept with exaggerated care up the winding stairway,

113

pausing briefly as she reached Jefferies' office. She tried the door. It was locked.

She did, just for a moment, consider what tale she could possibly spin should someone come across her there at that late hour, but the desire to get inside far outweighed any caution she might have exhibited in saner moments. It was quite amazing the range of skills one picked up from one's companions in an all girls' academy and equally amazing what a simple hair-pin, in the right hands, could accomplish!

The lock gave with a very faint click and Lizabeth slipped inside. She groped her way in almost total darkness across to the desk. Finding a lamp standing on it, she lit it, turning the wick down to its lowest.

The massive desk constructed of dark, heavily carved mahogany, dominated the room. All four walls were covered by book-laden shelves from floor to ceiling and, even viewed under the present circumstances, Saul Jefferies' office was very impressive indeed.

Still, Lizabeth wasted little time in admiration, but turned quickly to the documents stacked in neat, precise little piles on the desk-top. She discovered, much to her disappointment, that there was nothing untoward among any of them. It transpired that they were mostly invoices for hotel wares, some receipts, a memo or two and a few advertisement pamphlets.

Turning her attention next to the desk drawers, she found all but one, unlocked. Her hair-pin did not meet with quite the same success employed on this occasion, and she was just about to consider other means when, to her absolute horror, she heard voices in the hallway outside the office door. Footsteps were drawing closer and closer.

She looked about her desperately, seeking for a place in which to hide, remembering at the last second to blow out the lamp. She dived beneath the desk in almost the same instant the door to Jefferies' office opened. She frankly blessed the ego that demanded such a monstrous piece of office furniture.

'Could have sworn I locked that door,' she heard Jefferies' voice say to his companion. She held her breath, listening as he continued to stand in the doorway. He was obviously looking round the room, and she could almost hear his mind ticking over. He finally acknowledged that all seemed as he'd left it. 'I must have forgotten to lock up this evening; careless of me,' he muttered.

He crossed the room, each heavy footfall sounding like a death drum to Lizabeth, who wriggled into the darkest recess beneath the desk. Jefferies came to stand between the desk and its chair, only inches from her hiding place.

He rifled through the papers on the desk for some moments. 'Ah, here it is,' he exclaimed with some satisfaction.

'Well, what does it say?' the second man spoke at last, and she recognized him from her recent encounter as Shorty Styles.

'Damn code,' Jefferies swore, 'give me a minute.

There was silence so profound that Lizabeth felt sure the two men must hear her breathe. She drew up her knees to her chin, quiet as a little mouse hiding in its hole.

'Gaze says one hundred and fifty crates, delivered day after tomorrow,' Jefferies finally said, breaking into the quiet.

The other laughed. 'Good ole Gaze, workin' his butt off, ain't he.'

Jefferies did not echo the mirth. 'That's what he's getting paid for,' he snapped. He handled the paper with a thoughtful air. 'I sure hope Gaze isn't taking any chances, that's two deliveries to the Indians in as many weeks. Perhaps, you should ride down

116

to Sweet Water, and check it out. I don't want any foul-ups that end, not while I'm so tied up with the T.T. business here.'

He blew out the lamp and closed the distance between desk and door. The other followed close behind. 'Almost forgot, boss,' Styles said then. 'Saw that new school-teacher out walkin' in the moonlight.'

'At this hour?' Jefferies exclaimed.

'That's what I thought,' Styles replied. 'Could bear some watchin' maybe. Never can tell with females.'

Jefferies evidently nodded. 'Never you mind about Miss FitzMaurice,' he intoned, 'I'll take care of that lovely lady, you just concentrate on Sweet Water.' Lizabeth heard the key turn in the lock.

Just before the two men walked away, she heard Styles say in a muffled voice, ''Bout the T.T. boss, I got me a plan...'

Much to her regret, she was not to hear the full extent of Styles's plan for the T.T.

She waited a full hour before she dared creep from hiding. She had pins and needles in both legs by that time, and had some difficulty standing. While waiting for the circulation to return sufficiently to enable her to venture an escape, she searched again through the papers atop the desk. On this occasion, with Jefferies' words still ringing in her ears, the letter she sought took on a new significance. It was with acute disappointment that she finally acknowledged that Jefferies must have pocketed the document having read it.

She had no idea the degree of importance she should attach to her snippets of information, but she did appreciate the danger in which she had deliberately and, perhaps foolishly, placed herself. She shrugged metaphorically; actually she knew very little if the truth were known, but even that would have proved dangerous if Jefferies had discovered her beneath the desk in his office.

She crossed the room and bent to place her ear to the door, listening. All seemed quiet. She could hear the tick-tock of the big grandfather clock standing in the lobby, and the odd creak of timber as the house settled itself in the silence.

Well, she reckoned, now or never. Her hairpin yet again performed its task, serving her well. Peering outside with nerve-stretching care, she looked left to right, up and down the hall, her heart pounding. Nothing!

She took care to relock the door before leaving. She had no intention of arousing unwelcome and inopportune suspicions the following morning.

Reaching her own bedroom door, she slipped inside with profound gratitude, congratulating herself on her cleverness. She had a wonderful scenario all mapped out. Taggart would be completely overwhelmed in admiration.

Suddenly she found she was very tired. Her head dropped as she admitted herself not a little shocked at what she had just done. She had no need for caution now and she turned her lamp up full, as if its gleam could dispel the demons she had unleashed inside her head.

'Now, what time do you call this?' Styles's voice said from a chair over by the window. 'Ain't no fittin' example for a schoolteacher, comin' in at this hour.'

SIXTEEN

Lizabeth's head came up, her eyes were very dark and still. 'What are you doing here?' she demanded in surprisingly steady tones. 'How dare you come into my room like this. I shall inform Mr Jefferies first thing in the morning, do you hear?'

He grinned slightly. 'You do that,' he advised kindly, 'but meanwhile, maybe you'd like to inform me where you've been 'till now and, more important who with.' He studied the flat tips of his fingers. 'We can both talk to Mr Jefferies in the mornin' if'n you like.'

She took a deep breath, meeting his gaze with dignity, her eyes meeting his full on without flinching. 'That is no concern of yours, Mr Styles,' she retorted in her best schoolteacher voice. 'Now, I should like you to leave my room this instant.'

Her hand rested on the door-knob. It shook a little despite her efforts at calm. He stood up so suddenly that she gasped. Before she was fully aware of his intentions, he had crossed the room and stood beside her. He hit her that first time very lightly. 'Lady, I don't aim to hurt you if'n I can help it, but I wanna know where you was tonight and with who, do you understand?'

She nodded mutely. She was too angry to be afraid and her mind was ticking over at a furious rate. 'I was walking,' she said aloud, deciding that truth, even a diluted truth, was always the best policy.

He shook his head and sighed. He hit her

again, this time with more force. She gasped soundlessly; never having experienced violence of this kind before she stared at him in wild surprise.

'Where and with who?' His tone was so ordinary, so conversational that she could not quite believe what was happening.

'I was walking alone,' she said. He hit her a third time, hard. Blood oozed from her nose and her head was pounding. The room shifted alarmingly and she felt as if she might be sick. 'I was walking alone,' she reiterated desperately. She waited for the next blow. It didn't come. She glanced at him from beneath her lashes, attempting to gauge what he intended to do next.

'How come you know Taggart?' he said softly, watching her.

She dabbed at the blood which trickled down her chin. 'Taggart?' she repeated foolishly.

'Yeah, it was obvious when you two met earlier that you knew each other.' Her eyes flickered between puzzlement and hope.

'What's that got to do with this?' she said aloud.

He grinned, eyeing her as he might a child. 'Now, come on Miss Schoolteacher, you know all about it, so don't play no loco fool with me.' She was silent. He watched the light die from her eyes. She dropped her gaze and the long, black lashes rested in startling contrast against the deadly paleness of her skin. He reached out, flicked at a cut he had opened on her lower lip. She jerked away, her eyes blazing.

'I was with Taggart,' she flung at him. 'Is that what you want me to say? Well, I've said it, Mr Styles, for what it's worth. I've said it and now you can go.' She heard his breath hiss through his teeth. His eyes narrowed.

'Until this hour,' he snorted, 'it's near mornin'.'

It said much for her courage in the circumstances, but she actually managed to blush. 'You're a man of the world,' she ground out, holding tightly to the anger lest the fear should gain domination and destroy her. 'Need I spell it out, detail by detail?'

He stood up, paced the room's length, coming finally to the window where he stood looking down into the street below. Her nerves stretched with every moment that passed, while her heart raced and leaped.

'Why are you really here, Miss Fitz-Maurice?' he asked suddenly without turning.

'Here?' she parried.

He turned then, his face harsh and hard in the early light. 'In Boonetown,' he continued and she was reminded of another such question being directed at her earlier that night. Was it only a few hours ago that Taggart had stood here in this very room asking much the same question. It seemed as if it were another lifetime, so much had happened in the interim.

'Are you spyin' maybe for Taggart?'

She pushed an errant strand of hair from her face, noting inconsequentially that her best dress was spotted with tiny droplets of blood. 'Of course not,' she refuted the suggestion in a stout voice. 'How utterly ridiculous.' He waited silently while she continued. 'I came to Boonetown for no other purpose than to take up the position of schoolteacher, a position I might add, Mr Jefferies advertised. I happened to know Taggart from coming to the fort, and we merely decided that having met, purely accidentally, we should renew our earlier acquaintance. There's nothing more to it than that.'

Lizabeth choked a little on the last sentence, fear rising like gall in her throat. Styles crossed the room with exaggerated care and she stood up as he drew near. She mentally forced herself to meet his eyes. 'It's the truth; why should I lie?' she said, in as firm a voice as she could muster.

'Some of the boys went after Taggart tonight.' Styles changed the subject in that disconcerting way Lizabeth was beginning to recognize. 'They figured on savin' Mr Jefferies the trouble of runnin' him out of town.' Her eyes widened as the full meaning of his words penetrated.

'You mean they tried to kill him?' she said in shocked tones.

He grinned. 'Ain't nobody gonna grieve in Boonetown, 'ceptin' maybe you.'

He eyed her in a curious way. Taggart's woman! His eyes scanned the slender shape enhanced by the fitted evening gown and lingered at the hollow where the cloth clung hotly to softly rounded breasts. Taggart's woman here, his prisoner. That pleased him greatly. He flung her across the room with such violence that she bounced once against the dressing-table, hitting the side of her face. It swelled immediately and she lifted her hand to cradle the area in a dispirited gesture.

She couldn't think or plan or plead and she closed her eyes against the desperation. 'Reckon maybe you was tellin' the truth,' he said, rubbing his hands down the side of his levis, 'but don't go plannin' on leavin' town or nothin', you hear.' She nodded. He chuckled, causing her to to open her eyes warily. 'Damn, if this ain't a good joke. Wait 'till I tell the boys. Jefferies figurin' on sweet-talkin' you hisself and you Taggart's woman. Ain't that a good one.'

He reached for the door-knob as he spoke. 'I'll say good night, Miss FitzMaurice, but let this be a lesson. Don't you go gettin' no ideas or nothin'. Next time, I might not be so gentle with you.' He closed the door softly and she heard his footsteps recede. With considerable effort she walked stiffly to the door and shot the bolt. She then flung herself across the big, soft bed and promptly burst into tears.

SEVENTEEN

At about that same time, across the road in the Paradise, Lucky opened his eyes. He lay still for some moments reluctant to leave the warmth of his bed, but presently he pushed himself upright leaning back on one elbow, supported by his pillow. He found himself unnervingly disorientated. He could not recall the occurrence of the previous night or indeed how he had come to be sleeping in a strange bed in an unfamiliar room. He closed his eyes in confusion trying to get his bearings.

As memory returned they snapped open again. As if she had been waiting for him to notice her, Rosa quietly slipped from the room, ignoring his entreaty to remain and answer his many questions regarding the previous night's adventure. She returned moments later with a mug of freshly brewed coffee.

'Taggart'll be here soon,' she said, 'you'd best drink this down. He's a little late, it's gone first light,' she continued. 'Reckon he could've met with some trouble?'

'Naw, not Taggart, he'll be right along.' Lucky blew on his coffee, sipping the scalding beverage gratefully.

'You up in there?' Taggart's irate voice bellowed through the wood of the door right on cue. 'Near five-thirty; you plannin' on keepin' me waitin' all day?' He knocked again, louder. 'You comin'?'

Rosa hastened to unlatch the door, catching Taggart with his hand in mid-air as he prepared to knock a third time. 'Come in,' she said, 'the patient is much better this mornin', as you can see for yourself.'

Taggart threw a quick glance towards the bed. 'We best get movin', there'll be hell to pay when Jefferies discovers we raided the store.' As Lucky made no effort to vacate the bed, Taggart took the cup from his unresisting hand and impatiently flung the bedclothes aside.

Rosa was silently watching him. She said nothing but, taking the abandoned coffee cup from where Taggart had left it, she began to walk quietly towards the door. 'Where the hell you think you're goin'?'

'Downstairs,' she replied in an uncertain voice. 'Lucky's gotta get dressed ain't he?'

Billy grabbed Lucky's pants and shirt from the back of a chair, flinging them at him. 'Get dressed,' he ordered. 'Rosa'll admire the view from this here window, ain't got time for modesty.'

Rosa hesitated briefly before reluctantly taking up vigil by the window. She parted the curtains slightly to gaze absently down into the street below. Suddenly she frowned, leaning forward in sharp reflex. 'Billy,' she flung over her shoulder, 'reckon they've just discovered the missin' supplies. Ole man

Benedict's just comin' out of the store like the devil 'imself was on his heels. He's headin' right over to Jefferies' Hotel.'

'Damnation, knew we should have left last night,' Taggart ejaculated, closing the distance to the window in a single stride. 'Might make it still if'n we was to hurry.' He impatiently surveyed the room. 'Get some things together fast Rosa, you're comin' too.'

She frowned, biting down on her lip. 'Can't just up and leave,' she exclaimed stiffly, 'got me a job here, remember?'

Finally spotting the object he sought, Billy took a small travelling bag from beneath the dressing-table, pushing it into her arms. 'Pack up or come empty-handed, don't matter none to me.' Without waiting for her reply he turned to assist Lucky, who was having some difficulty getting into his shirt.

'Can't hardly raise my arm,' the latter grunted in a frustrated way.

Still Rosa hesitated. 'What the hell you think Jaeckell'll do when he finds out you helped Lucky here?' Taggart continued impatiently, pushing Lucky's hat down on his head in a determined way and handing him his boots. He ignored the grin the latter was attempting to hide. 'Jaeckell'll most likely figure that he had a right to beat you to death.' He crossed the room, opening the door carefully. 'You're comin' if'n I have to throw you over my shoulders and carry you, so get ready,' he gritted, in a tone she was fast coming to recognize.

She hurriedly flung a few possessions into the travelling bag. 'Ready,' she said breathlessly.

Taggart threw her an approving look. 'Good,' he replied briefly, peering out a second time. The hall was empty. 'All clear,' he said, 'let's go.'

Taggart's right hand went, of its own volition to the nondescript Colt resting on his hips. Each fibre of him was stretched taut, alert to the danger of their situation. Something in him waiting! Stepping on a loose floorboard, he tensed. The building groaned in the silence but all else was quiet. The atmosphere was heavy, brooding in the early light.

'This way,' he whispered gruffly, leading his two companions down the back staircase, out on to the alley to the rear of the building. He paused inside the doorway and listened. Finally assured that all was relatively safe, he beckoned Lucky forward. 'You take Rosa, get to the horses down by the livery,' he instructed in a low voice. 'I'll be along directly.'

Lucky nodded, a gleam in his eyes. 'You just remember, boss, Jaeckell's mine,' he said ominously.

Taggart grinned. 'Reckon we just might have to cut the deck for that pleasure,' he said with wry humour, 'but it's someone else I gotta find on this particular occasion.'

Rosa huddled in the shadows cast by the adjoining buildings. Her eyes in the gloom flicked from side to side, and she seemed agitated and strange. 'Come on,' Lucky encouraged, 'let's move out.'

She shook her head emphatically, hugging the travelling bag tightly in her arms. 'Ain't goin',' she mouthed.

Lucky scowled. 'Sure you are,' he retorted, but fell silent at a signal from Taggart.

The three escapees flattened against the saloon wall, and all held their collective breaths. The frantic thud of running boots on the sidewalk grew louder. As the racing men dashed past, the three hiding in the alley-mouth caught a fleeting glimpse of Jaeckell leading the pack. The man's face was ugly, both in expression and appearance. He ran stiffly, favouring his left side, and the extensive bruising on his bulbous

130

head was fast turning yellow. His nose was dreadfully misshapened. It appeared to have swollen overnight to twice its normal size.

'Reckon them boys is lookin' for us,' Lucky remarked, stating the obvious. He glanced at Taggart.

'Our time's run out,' the latter replied reaching past Lucky and pulling Rosa irascibly to his side, ignoring her cries. He frowned, his glance fleetingly resting on Jefferies' hotel entrance. 'Damn, damn,' Lucky heard him say beneath his breath, but wisely didn't pursue the subject.

With infinite care Taggart peered round the corner of the building, looking up and down the main street. People were already beginning to stir.

'Now,' he whispered urgently. He led the other two round the back of the building, keeping low, dragging a struggling Rosa behind him. They made the back of the livery. Their horses were waiting beneath the willows out back of the livery stable, that much was true, but so too were three or four of Jefferies' men.

EIGHTEEN

'Damn,' Taggart exclaimed, dragging his companions into the hasty concealment offered by a derelict shed conveniently situated close to the livery stable.

'What we gonna do now, boss?' Lucky asked, scratching his head. He was just spoiling for a fight and appeared to have all but forgotten his recent injuries. He took his Colt from its holster, spun the chamber and checked it was fully loaded. 'Reckon them *hombres* got us corralled here. Jaeckell'll be along shortly with the rest of the bunch, you'd best think fast, bossman.'

Taggart peered through the cracks in the decaying timbers. Drawing back, he ran a hand across his face, frowning irritably. 'We sure as hell can't stay here,' he remarked sourly. 'They've got us bunched up, snug as fleas in a bear skin.'

He bit his lip contemplatively. 'You reckon we could take 'em, if we was to make it to the stable without them spottin' us?' he asked quietly.

Lucky peered through another crack, measuring the distance. 'Ain't much cover,' he muttered in a thoughtful way, 'worth a try though.'

Rosa began to whimper. Her hands still gripping the travelling bag showed the knuckles white. 'You're gonna get us all killed,' she whispered desperately.

Taggart spun round. 'For Gawd's sake,' he muttered, 'can't you shut her up?' Lucky clamped one hand over her mouth, with his other he held her securely round the waist. She struggled for a time, finally subsiding into an uncertain silence.

Taggart went first, making the side of the livery stable without detection by those inside. Pressing an ear against the wall, he could just about hear their conversation. 'Gives me the creeps, waitin' round like this,' a voice he recognized as Styles said. Taggart heard a match strike followed by a scratching sound he couldn't identify. 'We'll be expectin' 'em,' a second man rasped, 'that's if they get past Jaeckell of course.'

A horse stirred in one of the stalls, stamped a hoof lazily. Taggart heard one of the men step closer to the doorway. 'Keep that damn fool head away from the door,' Styles snarled. The other shrugged, disappearing obligingly into the interior. Outside, only yards away, Taggart grinned without humour. Stepping backwards he failed, until the very last moment, to notice the pitchfork propped up against the wall, just behind him. He made a wild grab to prevent it falling. He missed!

'You hear somethin'?' one of the men inside the stable exclaimed. There was a shuffle of movement. Taggart lay flat, hugging the base of the stable wall, his gun drawn.

'Naw, ain't nothin',' a voice replied from the hay loft just above Billy.

'Gettin' mighty jumpy, Shorty,' the raspy voice snorted. 'Didn't hear nothin', did you Sid?'

The exterior door of the loft opened a mere fraction; a few blades of straw hovered in the lazy air, finally coming to earth just inches away from Taggart's hiding place. Uptop, Sid was evidently listening. 'Naw,' he repeated finally, 'ain't nothin' stirrin'.'

The men shuffled back to formerly held positions. 'Cigarette?' Sid called softly. Glancing away to his right, Taggart caught a quick glimpse of Lucky waiting. The sun glinted dully on the gun held in his hand. He waved to the younger man, gesturing towards the loft. Lucky nodded once and dropped from sight.

Taggart counted to fifty and then he stepped through the livery stable door. He flung himself off to the right, rolling in a neat, controlled movement, coming to his feet, gun already blazing. He caught a shiver of sound emitting from the tack out back of the livery and fired without aiming. There was a grunt of pain and a man fell, bringing all the tack down with him to the dirt floor.

Lucky's gun proceeded to blast in almost the same instant, and Sid, waiting above in the loft to ambush them, came through the ceiling, falling in a cloud of straw. 'All clear up here, bossman,' Lucky called in a remarkably cheerful voice. 'You want I should plug Shorty there,' he continued. 'Got me a clear shot from up here?'

There was a shuffling noise and Styles stood up, hands outstretched. Wordlessly, he threw his gun at Taggart's feet. Billy studied him with care; a lobo wolf, Styles was dangerous. Those colourless eyes were unsettling, never could tell what the man might be thinking, how he'd react. 'Ain't gonna get away with this,' he was saying, 'Jefferies got men all over.'

Taggart raked him with a single glance. 'Get her on to a horse,' he snapped, nodding towards the shed behind which Rosa still crouched. 'We're gettin' out of here.'

Styles's expression did not alter in the slightest degree. Those cool enigmatic eyes continued to watch Taggart, a small smile hovering round his mouth. 'You're a fool, Taggart, but I reckon maybe a brave fool,' he said, in a toneless voice, 'gotta give you that.'

'Someone comin',' Lucky intoned a warning, 'and he ain't friendly.' Acting on reflex, Taggart turned, firing from the hip. The man took the first bullet from Taggart's gun, the second from Lucky's. He spun round like a top, smashing into the stable door, the Winchester in his hand slipping from his grasp. The dying echo of the guns bounced off the timbers, and in the confusion Styles dropped from sight.

'We're gettin' out, now,' Taggart yelled, flinging Rose on to a saddle mare, slapping the animal's rump. The little mountain bred horse took off from a standing position, hitting full gallop before she had cleared the livery yard, the grey and Lucky's sorrel close behind.

Lizabeth watched events unfold, a helpless bystander. It was beginning to seem to her that she was destined to spend the greater part of her life following Taggart. She wasn't quite sure if she should be annoyed at this point, or simply amused. However, right then that was the least of her problems. The sight of Taggart galloping from the livery stable with Styles and his men in hot pursuit inspired, in addition to a wry amusement, something akin to foreboding in her. It appeared that she was trapped in Boonetown most probably at the mercy of Styles and with information which just might prove vitally important to the T.T. Her only guide out of town was fast disappearing in a cloud of dust even as she considered.

Her actual escape from the hotel had been accomplished without the least difficulty, Styles being preoccupied with apprehending Taggart and Jefferies also being obviously occupied elsewhere. Surprisingly, her borrowed duds, while of course too large, nevertheless concealed her identity. She had knotted a belt from one of her dresses round the waist of Taggart's pants so that they fitted reasonably snugly. Being quite tall, the length was more easily accommodated while the shirt had obligingly concealed the rounded contours of her shape. By the time she had rolled up her hair beneath the battered hat thoughtfully provided by Taggart, and pushed her arms into his jacket, she was unrecognizable as Boonetown's newest resident.

With Jefferies' men having gone, the livery stable she found on hasty investigation was empty. No one offered the least hindrance to her escape. She selected a bridle from the wall and heaved a saddle on to the back of one of the horses remaining in the corral. This task accomplished, she set off in the direction taken by Taggart and his companions.

She had never been out to the T.T., of course, and had only a vague idea of its location. Taggart, however, had spoken of it often and she felt as if she knew the surrounding country very well. For a time the trail was easy. If she listened intently and strained her ears she could faintly hear the sound of horses' hoofs in the distance. With a slight smile curving her lips she guided the little palomino mare she had selected towards the sound.

NINETEEN

The buckboard, with its welcome cargo reached the valley before sun-up that same day. With each hour that passed, those residing on the T.T. confessed anxiety for the safety of Taggart and Lucky. Zack, alone, shrugged off the need for concern, but fooled no one.

Finally, unable to bear the inactivity, the waiting, he took his horse uptop Look-Out Mesa. From that vantage point he could command not only the best view of the road from town but most of the T.T. valley. It looked particularly vibrant that morning, with all the various blues and yellows of summer flowers peering brazenly from among the green graze. The scene should have soothed him. It was going to be one of those warm, sweltering mid summer days. The lake to the foot of the valley already shimmered nebulously beneath the haze of heat, while a lone fish, more energetic than his companions, plopped to the surface. The ever widening rings spread across the mirror of water. Each blade of grass, each leafy tree was reflected there in all its perfection, each image clear and clean, so still was the water. It should have soothed, but it didn't, not that particular morning!

Off to the right the ranch buildings were just visible, small brown smudges against the northern pine belt. They nestled snugly at the foot of the mountain looking as if they belonged, and been there from the beginning. Zack walked the gelding carefully down the ascent from Look-Out Mesa, acknowledging the presence of his second son, Matthew who was keeping watch uptop the pass.

'Any sign?' he called, his voice echoing in the stillness, sounding unnaturally loud in the morning quiet. A small animal scurried away in the undergrowth, disturbed by the sound.

'Nope, nothin',' Matthew replied from above. His eyes followed the unidentified animal's progress as it careered downwards and then they rested on his father as the latter negotiated the path which wound itself round the pass and finally led perilously to the out-jutting boulder behind which he had made camp.

'Any coffee?' Zack dismounted as he

spoke, slipped the cinch's buckle a hole or two, and allowed his horse to seek whatever graze was available close to Matthew's look out post.

'Ain't there always?' the latter muttered in a dry tone belied by the twinkle in his eyes. He ambled over in his habitually lazy manner to join his father, indicating the small fire he had hidden behind the boulder.

Zack poured two mugs of the well-brewed coffee, handing one over with a nod to his son. Matthew grunted his thanks and the two men settled down to drink in companionable silence. Zack glanced towards his son in a pensive manner. Matthew was the most introverted of his boys, quiet by nature; he had in him a yearning for the lonely places. Zack figured when all this trouble was over and done, Matthew would go off seeking that virgin trail of his, right up into the far mountains, to the top of the world.

'What's happenin' down at the ranch?' he asked now, blowing on to his coffee. Zack didn't reply immediately. He chewed some of his tobacco. 'Buckboard's all but unloaded,' he began, and then stopped, remembering the expression on Taylor's face as he had helped unload. 'Just afore I rode out, Taylor was discussin' how best to go 'bout closin' up the North Pass. Reckons if'n trouble comes, that's our weakest spot.'

Matthew nodded, his eyes narrowed. 'Reckon he's right at that. It's wider up there; ain't so easy to hold against an attack, if'n it comes.'

Zack chewed some more. 'When it comes,' he amended. 'Taylor now, he figures they've enough dynamite to lay charges just at the foot of the mountain, should bring it down right pretty.'

Matthew took a mouthful of coffee, swirled it round his teeth. 'Sure would stop Jefferies' men from comin' through. This here pass is easy held, if'n we keep our eyes open and our guns handy,' he said. 'Should be no trouble, nope, none at all.'

Zack grinned mirthlessly. 'Son of a bitch ain't gonna get the T.T. as easy as he took over our spread.' He thought on that for a moment longer. 'Nope,' he repeated more or less to himself and with obvious satisfaction.

Again the two men fell silent. They were easy together and the silence was easy too. 'Reckon I'll take me a nap. Zack settled back against the boulder, pushing his hat forward over his eyes and proceeding to do just that. 'Wake me if'n you spot somethin',' he muttered, hearing Matthew soft-foot it from camp.

Taggart had set up a gruelling pace. It was as if having left Boonetown behind at last, he couldn't wait to shake the last of its dust from his boots.

'You'd best slow down some,' Lucky offered. 'Horses'll never last at this rate.'

Taggart pointedly ignored him. 'Keep movin',' he bellowed, shooting a withering look in Lucky's direction. 'Horses'll make it just fine.' The big grey, it was true, showed little sign of tiring as he ate up the miles with his long stride. Lucky was pleased to see how well his own sorrell kept pace, and Rosa's horse having the advantage of a much lighter load, was also holding her own. All three were fully aware of the men following. Lucky and Rosa wasted little breath in diverting Taggart from his course.

Coming into cover Taggart let the grey slacken his pace to a trot. It was obvious that he knew the territory well as he led his companions this way and that through the trees. After a very short time travelling in this erratic way, Rosa admitted herself totally lost. Behind them the pursuit sounded as though it were in difficulties, but it was apparent that they had not yet managed to lose them. Styles and the others just kept right on coming, but Taggart had managed to confuse them in a satisfactory manner.

Keeping well back in the trees and a careful distance behind Styles and his men, Lizabeth sat her horse and watched the antics of the men ahead. Taggart had indeed managed to confuse Styles and his men, but unknowingly, he had also managed to totally disorientate Lizabeth. She was forced to admit herself as lost as Rosa had earlier confessed herself to be. She pushed her hat to the back of her head and ran her hand across her face. It was growing increasingly warmer and she sipped gratefully at the warm, rather sour-tasting water in her canteen. It tasted good just then.

It was fully an hour later before Taggart and his two companions finally came to the mouth of the pass. Uptop, Matthew waved and Lucky returned the gesture. Taggart merely knee'd the grey forward and into the entrance. Lucky eyed him, wondering at the stern expression which closed him away from his companions. He was curious as to what might be the cause but catching the flinty glint in Taggart's eyes, he dared not ask.

'Riders comin'.' Matthew shook Zack briefly, his keen eyes having spotted the three incoming riders while still some distance off.

'Taggart?' Zack queried, coming to his feet with an ease that belied his age.

'Yeah,' Matthew replied, a grin spreading across his sombre features. He eyed his father anticipating the latter's reaction. 'It's Taggart 'n' Lucky; they got some female with 'em,' He flung the contents of yet another mug of coffee to the ground, reaching with his free hand for his rifle.

Zack spat. 'Trust Lucky,' he gritted in disgusted tones. 'Gotta have some female or other involved.'

Taggart's horse bounded forward as if suddenly spurred. Zack and Matthew climbed down to meet the incoming riders. In what seemed only an instant, Taggart was abreast of the two men. He flung himself from the saddle, spinning round with the force of his landing, the reins still in his hand. 'Howdy boys,' he yelled. He took coffee from Matthew with unspoken appreciation, not waiting for his two companions to dismount.

'Taylor get home all right with the supplies?' he demanded, in an impatient voice, gulping greedily at the hot coffee.

Zack nodded. 'All unloaded,' he said. 'Jess is plannin' a bakin' session like none you ever seen, there was so much sugar and such like.'

'That was Taylor's idea,' Taggart grinned faintly. He paused. 'The dynamite, that was his idea too,' he added.

'Yeah,' Zack replied, 'figured as much. The boys is down at the ranch this minute, plannin' a blastin'. They figure on closin' up the North Pass 'fore this mornin's done.'

'Good,' Taggart replied in a tense voice. He ran a hand through his hair, his face grey with exhaustion.

Zack had pointedly ignored his son's physical condition, with the exception of one speaking glance at Lucky's bandaged hand and bruised face. It wasn't until his glance shifted to include Rosa, wild and dishevelled following the mad dash from town, that he barked in disapproving tones, 'Who the hell is that?'

Lucky, recognizing the disapproval, glanced towards Taggart for help. Taggart, however, made an exaggerated show of having heard nothing, studying his nails intently. Lucky shuffled uneasily. 'This here's Rosa, Pa, she saved my life.'

Zack raised one eyebrow ever so slightly in sardonic disbelief. 'That so, Taggart?' he enquired.

'Well,' Taggart replied in dry tones, 'I reckon she did help some.'

Zack spat. 'Mmmm,' he grunted, 'seems like there's always some woman where Lucky's concerned. Don't figure that none.' He shook his head for emphasis.

TWENTY

'You boys rest up some,' Zack suggested, as he untied the seal-brown pony which was his favourite mount. 'I'll just ride on down, tell 'em you're all safe and more or less in one piece.' He frowned at his son who quickly dropped his gaze and shuffled uneasily. 'Best give some help with the blastin'. Like I said, you all rest up some, ain't no sense in us all bein' involved.'

Taggart nodded, leaning his back against the boulder, cradling his cooling coffee. 'Tell Taylor I'll be down directly,' he replied. 'Gotta talk to Matthew some. Figure it won't be long now afore Jefferies' men start makin' camp at the foot of the pass, boxin' us in. Even with the supplies, they'll expect us to run out of food sometime. Best start postin' double guards.'

Zack said nothing, merely swung himself up into the saddle and turned the seal-brown for home. Coming down into the lower valley he happened to come upon a herd of grazing horses. Taylor's black stallion, grazing among them, lifted his head sniffing the air. All the foals in the herd had the markings of their black sire. The stallion shook his head as he watched the man approach. He was magnificent and he knew it.

Zack screwed up his eyes against the glare of the sunlight. He lifted his battered stetson and wiped his forehead with the sleeve of his shirt. Shifting the wad of chewing tobacco to a new position, he paused to spit. Jesse appeared in the yard below him, her apron heavy with eggs still warm from the nests.

Spotting him, she called out, 'Any sign?' Her face was creased with the anxiety she had heretofore hidden from the men.

Zack smiled, pleased to be the bearer of good news. 'All safe and sound, Miz Jesse, bone tired and Lucky's got some fine bruises, but that's all.' He turned the seal-brown a little and then, remembering,

148

swung him round again to face Jesse. 'Got a visitor with 'em,' he amended.

Jesse's eyes widened. 'They have?'

'Yessum, some girl helped Lucky, so Taggart says. Maybe you're familiar with her, Rosa Lee, sings in the Paradise. Taggart reckoned it wasn't safe to leave her alone in town, not with Jaeckell all riled up like he was.'

Jesse smiled suddenly. 'Reckon it'll be nice havin' another female around the ranch for a spell. I've almost forgotten what it feels like to talk 'bout female things.' She wiped her face with her apron. 'Look at me,' she added, 'I'd best wash up some afore our guest reaches the house.' She ran her fingers through the unruly auburn hair which shone like burnished copper in the sunshine. 'If'n you're lookin' for Jim,' she continued with a smile, 'he's up by the North Pass with Killian, settin' them charges.' Zack nodded his thanks. 'Zack,' her voice halted his exit, 'you make sure they all take care, you hear.' Again he nodded, swinging the gelding round in a tight circle. He knee'd him to a canter.

Away in the mountains towards the north, blasting began splintering the morning's quiet.

At first it had seemed easy. Lizabeth had merely to follow a safe distance behind Styles and his men and they would obligingly lead her to the T.T. She hadn't considered her position any further than that, and it came as rather a shock to discover that once arrived at her destination, it was to prove no easy task to complete her half-shaped plans.

On finally arriving, she had reined in her horse and dismounted. The valley was just as Taggart had described and she stared appreciatively at the majesty of mountains, the peaks piercing the sky. Closing her eyes, she fancied she could catch the scent of pines and she smiled, imagining them circling the upper slopes within. Leaving the mare in a draw a safe distance from the valley mouth, she crawled forward until she had a reasonable view of the activity of the men outside. She watched in growing dismay as Styles and his men fanned out, obviously intent on setting up camp below the pass. Presently she caught the scent of burning wood as a camp-fire was lit. Before long the crisp smell of frying bacon and coffee wafted up towards her, reminding her forcefully that she had not eaten since the evening before.

After a brief consideration, Lizabeth led her horse further back into the rocks and ponderosa pines. She tethered the mare and set down to wait for darkness. She hoped that the men below so concerned with those on the inside would be temporarily un-interested in someone on the outside.

At last the day began to wane, the shadows grew increasingly long and the air cooled. Lizabeth stood up, stiff and not a little bruised from her encounter with Styles. She yawned and stretched and prayed a little. Somewhere in the night a coyote howled and she found that the sound echoed the feeling of aloneness she was feeling that night. She could smell rain in the air and she frowned as she swung herself uptop the mare. She spoke softly to the animal, running her hand across the horse's silky ears. The little mountain pony neighed and walked forward. Lizabeth guided her in a wide circle, carefully keeping to the darkness outside the camp perimeters. Every now and then she paused, head bent to one side, listening intently. At first it had seemed easy!

There was little moon, the shadows beneath the mountains were deep and dark. Uptop, Matthew unsuspectingly huddled closer into his heavy jacket, watching his brother, Killian kick gently at the fire. As Taggart had instructed earlier, the T.T. men now took the night watch in pairs.

'Reckon I'll take me a walk round,' Killian grunted. 'Never can tell with Jefferies what he might try.' He glanced up at the sky. 'Sure is a night for it, ain't it?

Matthew, too, looked upwards, grimacing at the cloud-heavy heavens. 'Damn, it's gonna rain afore mornin',' he said, with obvious displeasure. He stood up, stretched. 'Reckon I'll take me a little walk too, man gets sleepy sittin' round. You take yourself along that ridge over there.' He indicated a narrow path to Killian's left. 'There's a good view of the flats out below, but keep that fool head low, you hear? If'n you poke it up any, you'll be seen against the skyline.'

Killian grinned; his teeth flashed white in the darkness. 'I know that, little brother,' he said, 'what you take me for, a damn tenderfoot?'

Matthew didn't reply. 'I'm gonna climb down into the pass itself. Don't want no one tryin' to sneak up in the dark now do we?' With a quick wave he slipped from sight. Matthew was at home in the night and he had come to know the valley well. With little

152

difficulty he climbed down into the pass below, instinctively finding footholes in what was practically all sheer rock-face. Once or twice his levis scraped softly against the bare rock, and the sound seemed inordinately loud in the stillness.

Back deeper into the valley itself an owl hooted and, carried on the wind, came the sound of wild horses pushing through the brush. Ole Black was moving his mares again, the clever devil. Taylor'll have his work cut out finding them when it came time to cut the herd. Matthew grinned.

At first he wasn't sure what exactly was happening. He heard someone yell in a loud shrill voice, then gunplay. This was quickly followed by the sound of several horses coming up the ridge, horses coming fast and then there was a second yell. This time he recognized the voice as that of a woman and he frowned, totally at a loss.

Uptop, Killian let loose with a rifle. There was a grunt of pain in the darkness. A horse neighed shrilly. Matthew took the opportunity to scrabble back up the rock wall with more urgency than skill. Finding a ledge about six foot up he dug in. There was silence now, a silence so loaded with tension that it seemed set to split the seams of the night apart.

Matthew could hear himself breathe. He wondered about Killian's whereabouts, but he too appeared to have gone to ground.

Nothing happened for about fifteen minutes, the longest fifteen minutes Matthew ever remembered. His eyes ached from squinting down into the deep shadows below, and his hand ached from clenching round the trigger of his Colt. He'd sure feel more secure if'n he had his rifle to hand. But it had been too awkward to climb slinging a rifle along, so he'd left it just above, but out of reach. He could actually see it from his ledge and the sight of that rifle taunted him unbearably.

He contemplated making a grab for it, but before he could get set, it seemed as if all hell had broken loose. Killian's rifle spat several times in quick succession. It was obvious from the flashes in the darkness that he was changing position with each shot. This time an answering rally came from below, the shots whining off the mountain, one too close for comfort. Matthew, however, held his fire. It was obvious that those below weren't yet aware of his presence and for the moment that suited both brothers just fine.

His vigilance was finally rewarded. A boot scraped off stone somewhere below quite close. However, it was difficult to pin-point the exact spot, what with the echo between the pass walls and all. A shadow moved and Matthew fired blindly. A man's voice screamed and a shadow fell, rolling forward until finally coming to rest just below Matthew's ledge. A second shadow hastily retreated. Matthew fired twice at the figure, but knew he had failed to hit his target.

Again there was that awful still silence.

TWENTY-ONE

Matthew eased himself off the ledge. If'n they came again it would be all too easy to find him now that he had exposed his position. He hugged the mountain side and edged himself along nice and easy, reaching the outer mouth of the pass without incident. And then, for the second time that night, all hell broke loose.

The first indication was a horse and rider coming at full gallop up the rise. The rider's coat had come undone at some point in the night's activities and it flapped about as it caught the wind. Matthew stood up, taking careful aim.

Catching sight of him at the last moment, the rider jerked viciously on the reins and the galloping horse lunged forward, careering into Matthew. He was pitched aside like a rag doll, losing his gun in the fall. The horse was out of control, wild with the vibrations picked up during the mad flight up the mountain.

The rider, on seeing Matthew fall, stood up in the stirrups, swinging to the ground while the horse galloped on. Matthew saw him spin full circle, dropping on to one knee in an effort to regain equilibrium. The promised storm chose that particular moment to break, the rain lashing into their faces, adding to the confusion. Matthew lunged at the rider, bringing him to the ground with satisfactory force.

For a moment they struggled, the rider kicking and biting like a wild thing. Matthew felt the sting of a well-aimed punch before he finally pinned his adversary to the ground with an ease which caused his suspicions to crystallize. His breath hissed through his teeth, as a particularly stong flash of lightning illuminated the pale face framed by the long black hair which had come undone during the struggles.

'Damnation,' he yelled above the storm, 'you're a woman.'

She pushed him off and he let her go. 'I must see Taggart,' she yelled back. 'It's urgent; I must get into the valley.' She glanced back the way she had come. 'They're out there somewhere,' she said anxiously, 'please let's get out of here, it's dangerous.'

Matthew automatically reached for his gun. 'Damn, I've lost my gun,' he said in a worried fashion. He glanced round desperately, hampered in his search by the night and the blinding rain. 'Ain't gonna find it now, let's go, pronto.' He took her by the hand and practically dragged her into the pass. Sheltered somewhat from the full force of the storm's fury by the walls of the pass, Matthew paused. 'They ain't far behind, keep runnin', don't stop for nothin; you hear?'

She looked at him with wide, frightened eyes, but grinned gamely. 'I've won prizes for running,' she said, and set about proving her claim, matching the man stride for stride.

A rifle spat, its sound bouncing off the rock walls. Matthew wasn't aware he had been shot at first, not until the pain hit him and he stumbled. 'You've been shot,' he heard her scream.

'Ain't nothin', ma'am,' he murmured, 'keep runnin', don't stop for nothin'.' He pushed her ahead of him. 'Get goin',' he said, his voice sharp and commanding.

She refused to leave him, despite his entreaties. 'Where are you hurt?' she demanded, ignoring the speaking glance he flung at her.

'Ain't nothin',' he repeated, but it was obvious that he was beginning to feel the effects of his injury. He swayed against her.

'Put your good arm over my shoulders,' she commanded imperatively, and something in her voice made him obey without further protest. Then he was conscious of nothing, only the blackness of the night as he sank into oblivion.

The men following seemed to choose that particular moment to relocate their courage. They came at her in a pack, about three of them. She looked around wildly seeking some way to defend both herself and her unconscious companion. There was none and she felt once again that same sense of desperation she had experienced during Styles's interrogation.

It was over, all for nothing. She felt like crying, but hadn't the heart even for that. She closed her eyes, but they sprang open as she became aware of a sprinkle of stones which fell on her head from above her. She looked up. 'Catch,' a voice called from atop the same ledge which had earlier supported Matthew. Her father had taught her to shoot when she was no more than five years old. She caught the rifle without conscious thought, steadied the butt against her shoulder as he had shown her, and instinctively fired. She crouched low for leverage. The first man took her bullet in the gut and she didn't even flinch, the second Killian took, the third turned tail and ran.

Lizabeth sank to her feet. She refused to feel anything as she wearily cradled Matthew in her arms and waited while help from the ranch arrived.

It seemed like a long time, but in reality was no more than ten minutes until the buckboard arrived on the scene. Lizabeth, feeling somehow responsible for Matthew's condition, watched anxiously as the men loaded him with infinite care on to the straw-covered wagon. Matthew groaned a little, but didn't regain consciousness.

'Will he be all right?' Lizabeth queried, her

face showing the strain.

'He'll be fine, ma'am,' Lucky replied. 'Just fainted, that's all. Ain't nothin', bullet went clean through.'

Jesse was able to report some time later that Lucky's prognosis was correct. Matthew had lost blood, and would be feeling weak for some time, but the bullet had gone through and with care there should be no infection. In her opinion, she declared, he would live. The news cheered everyone considerably and, by way of a small celebration, the entire company, with the exception of Matthew of course, attacked Rosa's late breakfast of pan-fried steaks and potatoes with gusto. Zack even found room for two pieces of her apple pie hot from the oven.

Having satisfied his appetite, he began picking at a piece of meat which had lodged between his teeth. 'Reckon we best stick close to the house from now on,' he said, glancing round at those gathered at the table. 'Best keep on double guards at the pass; don't want no more surprises.' He was silent as he searched in his pockets for his chewing tobacco, but remembering where he was, he returned it rather furtively to his waistcoat.

'Jefferies' boys is campin' just below the

pass; been there since early this mornin',' he continued. 'Could've been a serious state of affairs, but we was lucky, damn lucky.' He thought on that a while, biting furiously on a fingernail. 'As if we don't have us enough trouble,' he added sullenly, 'we got that schoolteacher comin' a-hollerin' up the pass in the dark, tryin' to get her fool head blown off.'

He glared at the company in general. 'Thought Taggart had him more sense,' he finished resignedly.

TWENTY-TWO

Having left the breakfast-table earlier, Lizabeth was thankfully oblivious of Zack's strongly expressed sentiments. Even if she had overheard his derogatory comments, it wasn't at all certain that it would have mattered.

Taggart had offered that she be excused, indicating with a flinty nod that she should precede him from the dining-room. In silence he had held the outer door open and in the same intimidating silence they had walked across the ranch yard.

On reaching the corral fence they paused. Lizabeth eyed him from beneath her lashes, running her hand in a nervous way across the rough wood. Taggart was standing quite close and didn't, as she had expected, immediately move away. She licked her lips, her eyes dropped, clinging determinedly to his shirt front. He was mad as hell!

'Lizabeth,' he said in withering tones, 'I could murder you myself. You're the darnest fool of a woman I ever did meet. Did you even once consider the risk you took, comin' stormin' into the valley like you did?' She made no effort to reply, but bit down on her lower lip. That only seemed to infuriate him anew.

'Where were you this mornin'? I looked for you by the livery stable. 'Course you wasn't there.'

She tilted her chin at an obstinate angle. 'I was by the livery stable,' she retorted, 'just as you commanded, Mr high-and-mighty, never-wrong Taggart, but you were too pre-occupied shooting it out with Styles and, more or less, high-tailing it out of Boonetown to worry about me.' She drew breath, as angry as he and no longer able to hide it. 'So don't give me any of that where-were-you

162

stuff, you hear, because I won't stand for it.'

He eyed her in a punitive manner and she glared back. She came almost to his shoulder and she now straightened to her full height, tossing her head. 'Mr Taggart,' she began, furiously polite, 'you have no authority to lecture me. What I did was perhaps a little foolish; I didn't think of anyone being shot, but it was done with the best of intentions and I think you should acknowledge that and apologize.' She saw his mouth open and close as he struggled for a suitable reply.

'I'll be damned first,' he finally managed, a muscle throbbing just beneath his ear.

'Most likely,' she retorted with asperity.

She looked at him with narrowed eyes, as if appraising him. He shifted his weight a little, tilting his hat back so that the blondness of his hair was visible. Her eyes twinkled wickedly. 'You know,' she said in a thoughtful way, 'I'm not at all sure you deserve what I've done for you.'

He looked down at her, suspicion blatant in his face. 'There's more?' he gritted.

She shrugged nonchalantly. 'But of course,' she replied ominously. The suspicion in his face became satisfactorily more apparent.

'Let's see,' she mused, with the hint of a

smile curving her wide mouth, 'where should I start?' He grunted impatiently, but retained a determined silence. 'Should I begin by telling you all about stealing the horse from the livery, or perhaps at the point where I sneaked into those men's camp below the pass and cut their remuda loose, or should I merely dwell on the fact that since coming to Boonetown I've killed a man.' At this point she trailed into bitter silence. He could think of nothing to say and looked over her shoulder to a point beyond her, where the lake sparkled in the sunshine. He frowned, not liking the new bitterness which lay behind her speech.

'You shouldn't have come,' he replied flatly, 'told you not to.'

She shot him a fiery glance, her chin set at that familiar angle. 'Damn you,' she flung at him, her hands curled to fists by her side. 'Sometimes you can be a real son of a bitch.' She pivoted and would have left him, but his hand shot out detaining her. Her hair tickled his face as he bent forward. She smelled of horse and dust and hard riding and she had never seemed more beautiful. He touched her cheek with the tip of one finger. Her skin was soft and silky.

'You need a bath,' he said, drawing back.

Her eyes softened, meeting his and they both smiled.

'There's more,' she recommenced in a hesitant way. 'Last night after Jefferies and I had finished our night cap' – his face hardened in a way which pleased her, and she continued with more confidence – 'I was going up to my room. It was rather late. I'd gone for a walk, you see...' She risked a glance, but his expression gave nothing away. She paused before continuing again. 'I'm not sure why, but it struck me that I might be able to learn something useful in Jefferies' office, and I kinda, well, went in.' Absolute silence met her words, but his eyes had narrowed and she knew that he was angry again.

'I didn't find anything, not at first,' she pressed on hurriedly, 'but just when I figured that I'd sent myself on a wild goose chase, I discovered a locked drawer in his desk.' Taggart's face showed his eagerness. 'Did you know that Saul Jefferies has the most monstrous desk I've ever seen?' she added irrelevantly, her voice trailing off. His fingers closed round her upper arms and he shook her slightly.

'Lizabeth, I may truly murder you afore this day's out, do you hear? Never mind

Jefferies' damn desk, that's not important, what the hell did you find in it that's so all-fired important that you'd near get yourself killed gettin' into the valley?'

She licked her lips, savouring the moment to the full. 'Well...' she replied in dramatic tones, 'I was just about to pick the lock' – she had the grace to blush a little catching his grin – 'when I heard footsteps right outside the door, and the handle began to turn.' She paused for effect.

'Lizabeth,' he muttered warningly.

She rubbed her hands down the side of her borrowed levis. 'It was Jefferies and Styles, they were coming into the office. I scurried beneath that desk that's so unimportant,' she said, raising her eyebrows slightly, 'and hid. I was so scared I thought my heart would burst right there and then.'

'And...'

'And, Jefferies had a letter, or a message from someone called Gaze in Sweet-Water. That's in New Mexico. I know that because one of the soldiers at the fort mentioned it in conversation. Anyway, the message was in some sort of code. Jefferies decoded it for Styles. He said something about two deliveries in as many weeks, and Styles laughed and said that's what Gaze's getting paid for.' She frowned, sighing rather wearily. 'I can't make head nor tail of it all, I'm not even sure it was worth all the effort, and certainly not worth Matthew being shot, but that, for what its worth, is it.' At this point she stopped, her wide grey eyes seeking his.

'If'n I could find this Gaze,' he said almost to himself, 'maybe I could encourage him to talk some.' He grinned suddenly, a wolfish grimace. 'How the hell am I gonna get out of this here valley, Jefferies got us sewn up here like a cork in a bottle? Maybe we best let the others in on this, they might come up with somethin'.' He indicated the ranch house and she turned to comply, nodding her head in assent. He smiled at her then and the warmth and the approval she had long sought was there.

TWENTY-THREE

A stunned silence had greeted Taggart's brief summary of Lizabeth's adventures. Zack bit into his chewing tobacco and for once neither he nor Jesse noticed. However,

167

the problem of getting Taggart out of the valley went unsolved and continued to niggle away at each member of the T.T. as they went about their daily chores.

The storm had blown itself out and the day had proved itself bright and clear. It was one of those perfect summer days which fulfilled its season's promise. Zack viewed the distant mountain vista with pleasure, shading his eyes to look upwards into the blazing sun. He chewed appreciatively on his customary wad of tobacco and shifted his gaze to the meadows below. He grinned and spat.

There was something in the sight of newly mown hay which never failed to please him. Perhaps it was the solid look of the flat rows of hay which fell neatly and methodically as the mowing bar sliced through the grass, or perhaps it was the scent which filled the valley, the sweet, summertime scent of drying hay.

The jangle of harness and trace chains rang sharp and clear across the valley. Zack saw Taylor pause, lift his hat and mop his brow with his forearm, before again chirruping the team forward. Off to his rear, Lucky busily occupied himself in shaking the heavier rows loose so that they would dry that much easier in the hot sun.

Zack estimated that if the weather held, they could make up the cocks within the week, and then it would only remain to draw them in closer to the ranch complex and make up the rick. However, that was another day's labour!

He ran his hand across the back of his neck. Range war or no range war, work on a ranch was never done.

'They look like they could use this,' Jesse remarked, shading her eyes to watch the men below in the hay field. 'It sure is hot.' Zack glanced briefly at the basket of food she had prepared, catching the scent of newly baked bread and pan-fried steaks as it oozed through the red chintz cloth which covered the basket's top. 'It seems kinda funny, don't it, Jim down there directin' the hay makin' at a time like this?'

'Life's gotta go on,' Zack replied. 'Ain't no sense in waitin' for Jefferies to make his move, that ain't gonna feed the stock next winter.'

Jesse shifted the weight of the large blackened billy-can to her other hand. 'So you figure we'll be here next winter?' she said in a quiet voice. Zack merely grunted. 'Exceptin' you was all here, we'd have had to hire extra labour.' She nodded towards Lucky.

'Maybe,' he grunted, 'but Taggart wouldn't be up checkin' on the mountains neither, nor Killian watchin' the pass.' He frowned. 'I'll take that down, ma'am, no point in us all bein' out in the heat.'

She smiled. 'I was hopin' you'd say that.' She thankfully relinquished her burden and watched with a rather wistful look on her face as Zack made his way down to the meadow.

Taggart, having checked in with Killian atop the pass, walked the grey down into the pine belt, checking the range in general. The needles beneath the pines were so thick that they cushioned the sound of horse and rider. Only the odd creak of leather broke the stillness. There was nothing much stirring, not even a jack-rabbit, and Taggart felt as if there was no one else in the whole world except himself and the grey, isolated in the awesome grandeur of these mountains.

Below him through the trees, he could see the bright gleam of the lake and he smiled, remembering the fish he had caught there the first summer, and the cool feel of the water against his skin after a day's hot labour. The smile still lingered as he turned the gelding back into the sunshine. Time he set about helping the haymaking he figured.

Zack's arrival was welcomed by both labourers. Lucky flung his pitchfork down with abandonment and jostled his father good-naturedly as to who would have first choice of the basket's contents. Taylor completed one last length of the field, before guiding the horses towards the relative shade of some cottonwoods. 'Whoa up, now.' He pulled the team to a halt and jumped down to unhook the mowing bar. The horses immediately wandered off to munch on the sweet grass nearby. Some five minutes later Taggart had joined the others and there was silence for a time as each ate his share of Jesse's bread and steak, and drank her strong black coffee hot from the billy-can.

The sense of continuity, the feeling that this day's work was a mere continuation of nature's eternal cycle cheered Taylor and lulled him for a time to believe that Jefferies would see sense in the end and decide to leave the valley in peace. He closed his eyes and allowed the sun to play on his face.

Zack caught at his elbow, bringing him to full wakefulness. He indicated the faint curl of smoke rising into the sky from outside the valley and met Taylor's eyes with a knowing look. 'Closin' in, ain't they.' he said. He searched for his tobacco, but didn't immediately bite off a chew. 'Got me a plan,' he declared. All eyes turned towards him in a satisfactory manner. 'Ain't sure Lucky's gonna like it none, but I reckon we can get Taggart out of the T.T.' He bit off a chunk from the wad of chewing tobacco and began to chew industriously.

'Well,' Taggart prodded impatiently, as Zack failed to elaborate further. 'You gonna let the rest of us in on this fool proof plan, or are you just gonna hatch it like some damn cluckin' hen?'

Zack's grin widened. 'What you all reckon would happen if'n we was to let Lucky's sorrel loose down the pass?' He waved wildly in the general direction of the South Pass, his eyes on Taggart.

The latter rocked backwards on his haunches. 'I don't see...' he began, but Lucky interrupted with a loud laugh.

'I do,' he said, his expression almost exactly mirroring that of his father, the momentary likeness as fleeting as it was startling. 'You ever try catchin' that damn critter when he ain't of a mind to get caught?' he directed this at Taggart.

Realization was beginning to dawn. 'You reckon that that there sorrel'll keep 'em boys of Jefferies so busy that they won't notice me ride through their camp?' he asked in dubious tones, glancing ironically at Zack.

'Hell, I don't know,' Zack bit out impatiently, 'you got a better plan?'

'What you think, Jim?' There was a pregnant pause while all heads swivelled to gauge Taylor's reaction

'Might just work at that you know,' he said, having considered for some moments. 'Yeah, just might,' he added in a thoughtful voice, 'if'n you're willin' of course.'

Taggart raised an eyebrow. 'Of course,' he muttered in dry tones. Taking all as settled, Lucky stood up. He stretched lazily. 'Could take me near all day to catch that damn horse,' he grinned. 'Gonna have to leave the hay 'till another time, I reckon.' His eyes flickered over the gathering. 'Anyone wanna help?'

'Not me,' Taggart gritted, 'I've got enough trouble without bein' horse kicked.' Zack finally consented to help.

'He better not get hurt, Pa,' Lucky was heard to say as both men mounted up.

'Hell, Son,' Zack replied, his voice choked with laughter, 'what could possibly happen to that mean devil, most likely be too busy killin' some of Jefferies' boys. He'll have the time of his life, you'll see.'

TWENTY-FOUR

Breakfast next morning was a tense affair. There was nothing of the gaiety of the previous day; the shadow of range war seemed all too real in the pale, cold dawn light. Taggart's chair crashed back as he pushed it aside impatiently. He crossed the room and stood gazing through the open doorway.

Already the sun was warming. Its rays gleamed against the bare rock-face which towered protectively above the pine belt. The all prevailing silence was broken only by the familiar scrabbling of Jesse's hens in the yard, and by the lazy circling of the remuda in the corral off to the side of the bunkhouse. Taylor and the others were already mounted and Taggart watched them ride out, heading south.

With their departure, silence again returned to the kitchen. Only the clock ticking in the stillness and the hiss of the logs burning in the stove broke through Taggart's reverie. It was time to fulfil the promise he had made to Tom Lawson and to himself.

He huddled closer into his coat, mounted and urged the grey to a canter. The air held that sharp coldness particular to the dawn hour, and faint fingers of light were just showing behind the mountain tops as he left the valley. The sorrel, surprisingly co-operative, trotted behind.

At the mouth of the pass he drew rein. The light had strengthened considerably by this time and he thought he could detect some movement up by the lookout. He couldn't be sure. The Hales, with the exception of Matthew of course, and Taylor were up there somewhere he knew, preparing to offer diversionary gun-play should trouble start.

Catching some of his rider's tension, the grey danced uneasily. The sorrel began to tug in a determined fashion on the leading reins, the white of his eyes showing eerily in the post dawn light. Taggart sighed, feeling rather like a condemned man and yet did not once consider the alternative.

He could have turned the grey right there and then and ridden back down into the valley. Not one among his companions would have thought the less of him for that. But he didn't, he bent forward and unhooked the rope from his saddle horn. 'Here goes nothin',' he muttered as he swung it deftly above his head, controlling it with the ease of long practice. He brought it down hard and sharp on the gelding's rump, releasing him in almost the same instant.

The horse snorted indignantly and his ears pitched forward. He set his legs stiffly, flung his head up. In the next moment he plunged downwards, hindlegs swinging upwards and back in a vicious kick. He just missed the grey who had side-stepped in alarm. The gelding was all fired up and blazing. By the time he hit the camp below the pass he was like a demon straight from hell. A vicious temper allied with alarmingly accurate hooves and teeth quickly disposed of would-be captors with savage ease. The horse was thoroughly enjoying himself as Zack had predicted! He rose full on his back legs defying the scurrying and disorientated men to box him in. Taggart for the first time could empathize with Lucky's admiration of the animal. He really was a quite magnificently savage beast.

He knee'd the grey forward, leaving the

concealing shadow of the pass, quietly guided the horse through the mêlée. He tried to look as if they belonged. Once or twice the grey turned his head to regard the antics of the gelding, but on the whole he was apparently unimpressed. By now the sorrel had unsettled the camp's remuda. The tethered horses had begun to pull on the line, pawing the ground and tossing their heads in a restless manner.

'Hi, you,' one of the milling number grabbed Billy's leg. Taggart's hand dropped to his gun. 'Get a rope on that damn bronco, you hear?' the voice continued. 'Get him the hell away from that remuda. Damn 'im, he'll have 'em up and runnin' soon as spit.'

Billy walked the grey forward. 'Sure thing,' he replied in a gruff voice, pulling his hat forward. 'I'll get 'im.' He sketched a brief wave, reining the gelding round in a tight circle. The man took two quick steps backwards.

'Shoot the son of a bitch,' he added in an increasingly agitated voice, waving madly towards the sorrel as he spoke.

'Ah hell,' Taggart muttered savagely as he unsheathed his rifle and took careful aim. His bullet kicked dust between the sorrel's forelegs, causing him to rear furiously. It most probably saved the animal's life, as the men had by this time begun to reorganize, but his action drew what Taggart could only describe as a murderous look in lieu of gratitude. Still, it had the desired effect. The sorrel took off at full gallop, the entire remuda close behind him.

'Damn 'em,' a second man spat out. He flung his hat to the ground and stamped on it in blind fury. Others began to run after the fleeing horses in a futile attempt at catching them. 'I'll get 'em,' Taggart bellowed to one in particular.

Perhaps there was something about the way he sat his saddle that was peculiarly his own, perhaps it was something in his voice when he spoke, perhaps Taggart's luck just ran dry... Whatever the reason, with the sorrel's exit the men's attention swung to the only one among them still mounted.

'Hi, that's Taggart.'

Billy felt rather than saw figures dash forward to pull him from his horse. In desperation he slashed viciously to left and right with his rifle butt. The grey lunged forward, breaking free in almost the same instant that T.T. rifles began firing from the relative safety of the mountain above. Taggart lay low

Indian fashion, across the horse's neck, bullets whizzing past too close for comfort. Gradually the morning emptied of the sound of guns and Taggart realized, with something akin to disbelief, that he had actually escaped and, more to the point, was still alive.

Several hours later he built temporary camp. A long belt of cedars and pine grew just above him, extending for several miles. Beyond them the natural rock formation offered numerous side canyons and a positive labyrinth of trails. He wrapped some of Jesse's bread round a piece of salted bacon and ate in a thoughtful way. He had a lot to consider!

Jefferies was a damn clever man and not to be underestimated. In the wake of Lizabeth's flight to the ranch there was every possibility Jefferies would put two and two together and come up with five. Taggart's mouth tightened. He'd get the proof Tom Lawson wanted, even if he had to kill Gaze in the process.

The following days were hard, both on Taggart and the grey. They travelled fast, making dry camps, resting only for brief periods. He pushed on relentlessly, building up as much distance as possible between those he knew were following. He was by nature a careful man, and he took care to keep off the horizon, following the washes and low areas. He knew the country, knew where to hide and where to find water. Each day at noon he rested. He was profoundly glad of any shade the terrain could offer, and that was scant and scarce enough.

Coming across a smallish grove of cotton-woods round noon of the fourth day, he dismounted wearily. He had come quite some miles into Apache country and he was keyed up with the knowledge. Nothing much stirred in the debilitating heat. The sun filled the sky as it hovered above the desert and rocks. It was peaceful though in the shade of the cottonwoods. Somewhere quite close a bee hummed as it busied itself gathering pollen. Taggart chewed on some jerky and followed its progress with idle interest as the insect continued to flirt from flower to flower. Finally it flew upwards towards a second smaller grove just above his camp. A jack-rabbit even peered from behind an outcrop of rock some feet from Taggart's resting place. He sniffed the air delicately before bounding upwards, also towards the second grove of cottonwoods.

Suddenly that rabbit veered off the

straight line it had previously been following. It veered off quickly and abruptly and without explanation.

Then that all-prevailing silence, no movement, no sound.

TWENTY-FIVE

For a long moment Billy didn't think. He simply remained perfectly still, the jerky forgotten in his hand. He stared without blinking at the spot from which the jackrabbit had fled and waited for something to happen. As the moment passed and the stillness of the spot remained unshattered, he moved. With infinite care he crawled forward, keeping low. His hand slipped to his Colt as he edged closer to the upper grove of cottonwoods.

He reached them without incident and was disconcerted, but not terribly surprised, to find nothing. He crouched low, his head to one side, listening with an intent expression on his face. There was nothing, except the angry twittering of two birds as they exchanged insults somewhere above him in the rocks.

Billy tightened his grip on the Colt, feeling the palms of his hands grow wet and slippy with sweat. This was Apache country and he was alone in dangerous territory. It had been foolish to come into the rocks; he turned suddenly, overcome by the urge to run from the place. As he turned to leave, however, something in the dust caught his attention. He bent quickly but not before he threw a searching look around the area. The object which had caught his attention was a small suede pouch which was covered in a fine film of yellow dust from the ground. Billy's eyes continued to dart from side to side, scanning the immediate area as he examined the pouch with his hand.

He knew its contents without opening it. He had seen such pouches before. He untied the beaded threads holding it closed and, as he had expected, its contents proved to be a lucky fetish, an object much prized by Indians as having magic properties which could ward off evil spirits and bring its wearer good luck. The fetish in Billy's hand was a small, rounded piece of blue turquoise. It was very pretty as it nestled there in his palm with the blue of the sky reflecting in its jewelled contours.

Moccasin tracks marked the sand close by the spot in which the pouch had rested. They led upwards for a time, and then disappeared without trace. The urge to leave escalated to uncontrollable heights and Billy made it back to the grey in a fast trot. He mounted up and left hastily, but all the while exercising caution. He carried his Winchester across the saddle. The barrel grew searingly hot in the noon sun and he covered it loosely with his coat protecting it from the effects of too much heat. He was expecting trouble and if it came, he wanted it to find him waiting.

It was as if the land itself shared his tension. The sun seemed too big and too hot in the sky, and the rocks threw shadows across the sandy soil, each one seeming to move as he approached. The grey ate up the distance with long, easy strides and, as the cottonwood groves fell further behind him, and no riders wearing war paint put in an appearance, he gradually relaxed, but he still carried the rifle across his saddle.

Two days later – two days travelling, two nights without sleep – still nothing un-toward had occurred. Perhaps he had been mistaken after all, but he dared not take that chance. A lone white man riding a good horse was too tempting a prize for a raiding party to be allowed to slip away so easily. He'd probably have killed two, maybe three Apache before they'd have gotten him. In the end he'd have died one way or another. He could only have hoped that it was quick!

By the time he had reached the seep at Red Rock, Billy's water had long since gone. He approached the spot cautiously about an hour after sun-up. He figured if there was a raiding party in the area that they too would undoubtedly know of the seep and most likely visit it.

It was dry!

The earth round about showed signs of recent activity. There were several animal prints, mostly rabbits. But among the other familiar prints, Billy spotted that same moccasin footprint. Someone had quite recently used the seep and that made Taggart nervous as hell, but he couldn't travel much further without water and Red Rock was the only one he knew of for several hundred miles. It would take an hour or so for it to replenish itself. He had little choice but to settle into the rocks close by and wait for the hole to fill up again. The horse was tired, needing rest and water. If it came to it, so did he!

Now and then, he sat up and watched the grey. Mountain bred horses were first-class watch-dogs. Billy was familiar with its every gesture and if there was anything out there, the gelding would know. Watching him, Billy too would know. He chewed on some jerky and drank a little of the muddy water which was slowly seeping through the sandy soil. He was glad of it despite its unsavoury appearance. Billy encouraged the gelding to drink before finally mounting up to leave. A scouting party thirsty for water might just chance to come along after all. Blond scalps, being rare, were much sought after by Apache warriors. Billy's was sure to cause quite a stir if it should come to be swaying in the breeze outside some brave's tepee.

Rider and horse had covered less than six yards when the grey suddenly came to a dead halt. His ears were pinned forward, his head held slightly to one side in enquiry. If he glanced over his left shoulder Billy could still see the hole in the ground where the water seeped through.

In spite of his urgings the horse continued to stare fixedly at a small clump of bushes just off to the left of the trail. He stubbornly refused to advance. He wasn't acting scared, just curious. Whatever was in those bushes obviously wasn't perceived as being a threat. At his rider's continued insistence the grey finally took a single step forward, nostrils extended, before again coming to an uncertain stop. This time he positively refused to advance further despite Billy's alternating threats and coaxings.

'Damnation,' Billy exclaimed at last, his patience taxed to its limits, 'it's just some small critter, you fool horse.'

He tightened his knees and the horse obediently walked a little closer to the offending bush. He was still curious and uncertain as he bent to sniff the branches. A small, almost discernible quiver ran through the branches and the gelding started away violently. He tossed his head and snorted. Billy knew horses, how they acted when they were alarmed and how they acted when they were just plumb stubborn. He knew the grey better than most. If the gelding had any single fault at all it was his damn curiosity.

'Hell,' he bit out viciously as he dismounted.

Although not unduly concerned, he nevertheless slipped the Colt from its holster and held it ready as he pushed the thorny branches aside. In the following seconds he registered two things. Firstly, his suspicions were proved correct after all – he had been followed. Secondly, his pursuer was not the warriors he had feared, but none other than a thin, hungry Apache boy, not more than nine or ten years old.

After the initial shock had passed, they studied each other in silence. Billy frowned as he studied the boy. Judging from the angle at which the bone protruded through the skin of his left arm, Taggart was fairly sure that sometime during the two previous days, the boy had somehow managed to break his arm. Despite this injury, and in spite of the fear darkening his eyes, the young Apache glared out unflinchingly from beneath the straight dark fringe of hair.

He wore only a loin cloth and a pair of worn moccasins. His long straight hair fell almost to shoulder length. A band of otter skin circled his head and he wore a single string of beading down his thin chest. Billy haunched down to the boy's level.

'Your arm's broken,' he said in the boy's tongue. He received no answer, only the briefest flicker in the dark eyes indicated that the boy had understood. 'I will fix it,' he continued, moving a little closer. The boy shifted awkwardly, his face tight. 'I am your friend,' Taggart tried again. 'I will not hurt you, but your arm must be set or it will go bad. Do you understand?'

The boy considered this, his eyes following Taggart as he watched him break off two sturdy branches from a near by tree, testing them for straightness and strength. Billy saw the curiosity in the dark eyes and grinned. Indians were near as curious as that damn grey horse. Perhaps he could use that to lure the boy from hiding.

'These are to hold your arm,' he explained in conversational tones, as he cut the wood to lengths of equal size with his hunting knife. He turned away a little from the boy, but was pleased to see from the corner of his eye that the young Apache had moved forward ever so slightly. 'You want me to show you how to fix a broken arm?' he continued to coax. Still the boy hesitated, but Billy was confident he was winning him over.

As the boy attempted to gain his feet Billy reached forward in a reflex action to assist. The boy jerked back so violently that pain jabbed right through him in a vicious ripple. Sweat dampened his small face but he stoically uttered not a single sound. His head fell to his chest, and it was several seconds before Billy realized that the youth had passed out cold.

TWENTY-SIX

It was several hours before the boy came round again. Billy had strapped his arm to the splints and the pain had dulled somewhat. Taggart gave him little time to rest, anxious to keep moving. He didn't like the territory nor the implications of having the boy along.

Each day took them deeper into the New Mexican territory, through the arid, rugged isolation of numerous steep-walled canyons and serrated mountain trails. To the north the desert, ringed by distant ridges shimmered in a haze of heat. Taggart thought frequently of the folks back on the ranch. Had he made the right decision in coming out here to this wilderness when perhaps he could have been more effective helping to defend the valley?

For all he knew Jefferies could have already penetrated the valley's defence. His greatest fear, however, was for the safety of those he had left behind. Sometimes he felt almost as if he had deserted them, and it took some thinking through before he could absolve himself of that charge. Conscious all the while of time passing, he wished that he could see where it all might end.

As it happened he couldn't have foreseen the half of it.

They had picked up his trail at the seep and tracked him to his first noon camp. They had not come for water, although that was welcome, they had come seeking the boy.

Evidence of Taggart's passing obviously disturbed them, particularly when there was sign enough to indicate that he had left the seep taking the boy with him.

Black Eagle, the leader of the party, bent to touch the ashes which were all that remained of Taggart's small fire. They were almost cold but told the Apache chief all he needed to know. He swung himself upright in the easy unconscious way of one who is in the prime of physical condition. His face was dark, broodingly inscrutable as he turned towards the south-west. The sun glinted on the eagle feathers threaded through his black hair. This was a badge of honour and he wore it proudly. He was quite tall for an Apache, almost as tall as Taggart, and he carried himself with that same inherent grace. He wore only buckskin leggings, breech cloth and moccasins. His naked torso gleamed in the sunlight flirting through the cottonwoods. A small pouch, similar to that worn by the boy, hung round his neck.

He shaded his eyes as he glanced towards a belt of ponderosa pine and then towards the mountains beyond. There was something disturbingly ferocious in his expression.

'We go,' he commanded in guttural tones.

Taggart reached the ponderosas about dusk. He guided the horse into the gathering gloom beneath the pines, finally drawing him to a halt and indicating to the boy that they would rest up some. The boy was tired and much weakened by the day's ride. Taggart eyed him silently. He would not risk a fire, but he gathered some branches and made the youth a makeshift bed. In the quiet of the darkness hours he dozed fitfully, never quite asleep, but resting a little nevertheless.

During the course of that day they had come across a small hunting party. Taggart had held the grey back in the undergrowth. The horse had seemed to understand the necessity for quiet and had stood still, his ears pushed forward watching the riders pass. The boy had tried to call out, but Taggart's big hand had clamped across his mouth in almost the same moment the thought had crossed his mind. 'You call out,' he had whispered into the boy's ear, 'and I'll most likely break your other arm, you understand?' The boy nodded mutely, believing him.

Taggart studied the hunting party as it continued on its course. The Indians were obviously out in a search for food. They were not painted for war. Taggart figured that there was a village somewhere in the area, and he wondered if perhaps the boy belonged there. However, what really caught at his interest were the new Winchester rifles carried by some of the warriors. The barrels gleamed shiny in the sunshine. Taggart played briefly with the idea of back-trailing the party, but figured that that was not only dangerous, but pointless. It was unlikely that he would learn much and most likely would only find himself in deep trouble.

Somewhere in the woods an owl hooted, a second replied, recalling him to the present. The boy stirred on his bed of pine needles, a peculiar expression on his face. He glanced slyly towards Taggart who was just visible by the big boulder sheltering their camp. His head had dropped on to his chest but the boy had a feeling he wasn't sleeping.

Again an owl hooted, this time much closer to the camp. Again a second replied. Taggart's head shot up. He suddenly put his hand to his mouth and echoed the owl's call. He leaned further into the shadows and listened. The boy fingered the little suede pouch which Taggart had returned to him and which was once again circling his neck.

He could not fathom this white eyes, who was not as he had been led to expect. He somehow challenged all preconceived notions and turned certainty into a kind of doubt. Acting in that instant more on instinct than anything else, the boy bur-rowed deeper into the pine needles and remained mute.

The woods, which should have been alive with nocturnal sounds seemed unnaturally silent, as if waiting and watching. Perhaps it had been that very silence which had first warned Taggart.

He had not slept in as many days and he was running almost exclusively on adren-alin. While the boy had slept he had walked the grey some distance down into the rocks and tethered him there. He had tied leather pads to the gelding's hoofs and exchanged his own boots for a pair of soft moccasins. Back in camp he had stood for a long time just on the perimeter, listening motionless but finally abandoning his vigil to hunch Indian-fashion by the boulder. Patiently he had waited for that first owl call, somehow instinctively knowing that it would come before morning.

The boy had not stirred but Taggart had a feeling he too was awake. He crawled over and touched the youth gently on the arm. For once the young Indian did not flinch from the contact. 'Your people are out there in the night; you are safe. I will leave you now.

The boy's oblique eyes gleamed in the darkness. 'It is my father,' he spoke for the first time, in a soft voice, the pride of generations in its tone. 'Perhaps he will kill you.'

Taggart grinned without humour. 'So, you can talk after all,' he muttered. The boy watched sullenly as Taggart regarded him for a moment before soundlessly disappearing into the night.

Out in the darkness, he slung his rifle over his shoulder and slipped his hunting knife from its sheath. He gripped it between his teeth and with infinite care edged forward

194

on his belly through the scant undergrowth. Once or twice he thought he detected fleeting movements quite close, but he couldn't be sure. Apache were like ghosts. They came through the woods so silently it was frightening and they could hide in places that seemed downright impossible. He could hear himself breathe in the quiet. The soft scraping noise he made as he brushed against hidden rocks sounded dangerously loud to his straining ears. Eventually though, he made the lower slopes and the relative safety of honeycombed rock crevices – and the grey!

TWENTY-SEVEN

Suddenly he paused. He thought he heard something. There was someone or something shuffling round in the rocks quite close. He reached instinctively for his knife. Damn, Indians weren't supposed to fight at night; feared to lose their way to the happy hunting grounds or something. Hell, another fool notion not worth spit! He tensed as the shuffling drew closer.

He wasn't sure who was more shocked, he or the hunting desert fox when they eventually came face to face. The animal stood as if stunned for a split second before high-tailing it back the way he had just travelled.

It was too dangerous to remain in the mountains until sun-up. He'd best move while darkness held. Come sun-up he'd be trapped for sure. He led the gelding downwards, zig-zagging as best he could, the odd creak of leather the only sound. The horse seemed to sense the necessity for caution and he stepped out needing little encouragement. Just before dawn he tethered him again some distance from where he himself intended to rest up. Then he squirmed into an opening between two large boulders and curled up. With a sigh he dropped the rifle from his shoulder and rested it across his knee. He arranged spare shells in a neat line close to hand and checked that his handgun was fully loaded. It was to be a long day!

The evening sky still retained a little of daylight when he finally decided to come out of hiding. There was just about enough light left to make the travelling a mite less hazardous. He edged forward until he was just outside the opening to his hiding place. He paused to listen, his head bent slightly to one side. Satisfied, he moved out silent as a big cat over the rocks. He paused frequently, getting his bearings and listening. Nothing seemed to stir. The world waited.

It got progressively colder as the sun dropped even lower behind the mountains. The night was inky blue, the shadows deep and long. By the following morning he figured he'd escaped. Heat, even at that early hour already radiated off the rocks and gave some indication that the temperature was yet to soar. Sweat trickled down his face and clung uncomfortably between his shoulder-blades. He hardly noticed. A hawk hovered overhead, motionless in the early sky. Evidently sighting something fool enough to move on the desert floor, it dropped from its elevated vantage point like a stone from heaven. A small animal squealed somewhere below and then there was nothing.

Round about noon he found himself some shelter from the sweltering heat. His canteen was about half full but he drank sparingly, sharing a little with the grey. Never could tell when he'd next find a water hole. Glancing back along the way he had come, the canteen halted halfway to his mouth.

On the horizon, clear as day, six Apache sat their ponies.

For what seemed an eternity, but was in reality only moments, the tableau remained thus. No one moved. The very faint breeze coming down off the higher slopes caught in the ponies' manes and in their riders' long hair. The sun shone mercilessly down and that hawk hovered again in the cloudless sky.

One of the six then left the party and began to approach Taggart. The unsaddled paint walked slowly but inexorably closer, the rider zig-zagged to indicate that he approached in peace. His five companions held their positions on the horizon. It appeared to Taggart in those moments that everything seemed to be happening in slow motion.

He could remember vividly long afterwards each nuance of the approaching Apache's face, the yellow paint adorning the high cheekbones, the black, sleekly oiled hair, the beaded headband, the proud haughty tilt of his head. There was an unexpected, but unmistakable look of the boy in the man's features. Taggart felt almost as is he were looking at the boy full grown. He came to within a yard of Taggart and drew rein, sitting his horse in silence. His dark eyes studied Taggart. Billy met the man's eyes full on and waited for him to speak.

'I am Black Eagle, father of Little Bear.'

Taggart nodded. He had guessed as much. 'He broke his arm. I tried to fix it.' He glanced upwards towards the horizon. 'Little Bear is not with you?'

Black Eagle pointed back towards the mountains. 'He waits for us. We will take him home soon. He is safe.' There was a pause while he formulated his next sentence. 'I thank you,' he said then, very simply, neither meek nor arrogant. 'You have given to me my son. I will speak your name with honour, Taggart, as will my braves. I have willed it so.' He raised his staff, the feathers which trimmed it fluttered with the movement. 'Come, ride with me a little so that my braves will see you are my brother and they will not harm you.'

As they rode, Black Eagle told him of his village and of the welcome which he would find round the cooking fires. Taggart remarked on the Winchesters he had seen some of the warriors carry while out hunting earlier, but Black Eagle refused to be drawn on the subject. Taggart was wise enough not to press.

'I have a friend,' he ventured, 'in Sweet Water. His name is Gaze.' He studied the Indian's reaction closely, noting the faint tightening of his mouth.

'I know of no one of that name,' he replied in dismissive tones, 'and now we talk of other things.'

And so it was that Taggart finally came to Sweet Water.

Sweet Water for all the beauty in its name, was nothing more than a collection of crude dwellings clustered untidily round a centrally located well. The settlement had sprung up within the shadow of Fort Lauderdale and its inhabitants looked towards the fort as their protector in a hostile environment. The well, which was its main source of water, sometimes dried up in the height of summer it was true, but generally could be relied upon to supply the needs of the dwindling population roundabouts.

Sweet Water commanded views of rugged isolation. There was nothing as far as they eye could see, except the rose-coloured desert and the red mountain formations. The odd patch of mesquite, cat-claw and yucca salvaged the scene from absolute monotony.

Taggart glanced round as he rode down the single street. Curious eyes followed his progress and he caught fleeting glimpses of pinched brown faces as their owners hastily withdrew into the gloom of inadequate shantytown dwellings. His eyes were hungry for sight of anyone who could possibly be Gaze. As it happened it was to be several days before he was to meet the man.

He dismounted in front of the saloon. Immediately a small Mexican boy materialized by the horse's head. 'Water your horse, *señor*,' he offered brightly.

Taggart studied him in a considering way. He smiled suddenly. 'Here,' he said, tossing a coin into the air. The boy caught it deftly, a wide grin split his face.

'I'm looking for a man,' Taggart continued, in an uninterested way, 'his name is Gaze. Know 'im?'

The boy's eyes had a knowing look. 'You are a friend of Señor Gaze?' He queried, not exactly cautiously but not openly either. Taggart lifted his hat and rubbed inside the band with his bandanna.

'Might be,' he muttered. He looked up. 'Might not.'

After a moment's consideration the wide grin reappeared. 'Señor Gaze he likes to spend time in Manuel's.' Taggart tossed a second coin in the boy's direction. 'But he is not here today, he is away.'

'Away?' Taggart echoed.

'Yes, *señor*, he is doin' the, how you say, the business, you understand?' He stopped as if fearing he had said more than he judged wise. 'I will water him good,' the youngster rushed on, anxious to change the subject and to assure his benefactor of his reliability despite his reluctance to assist in other areas. Taggart did not pursue the topic and the boy was obviously relieved. He was satisfied with the original transaction, having first bitten on the coin to ascertain its authenticity and did not want to endanger any further possibility of a repeat. However, he would venture no further conversation. He led the grey then towards the centre of the town square and the well with the sweet water, casting a single searching glance towards the tall gringo with the golden hair.

Taggart had remained standing in the dusty street by the bottom step of the *cantina*. His head was thrust up, his eyes closed as he allowed the sun to play on his face. He'd have Gaze soon, one way or the

202

other, he could feel it in his gut!

His entry into Manuel's *cantina* caused quite a stir. Not merely because he was a stranger in town but also because there was something about Taggart which generally demanded folk take a second look. He chose a table situated in the far corner of the room, facing the door. His back rested against the wall. The barkeep hurried over to his side. 'Tequila, señor?' he queried nervously.

Taggart's face was shaded by the rim of his hat. His eyes surreptitiously raked the occupants of the room. 'Beer,' he said in a low voice. For some reason, the barkeep seemed nervous. He started, his eyes met Taggart's in an anxious way.

'Beer?' he repeated.

Taggart deliberately pushed the stetson to the back of his head. He did not speak, reaching into his breast pocket for the makings. The silence lengthened. Taggart rolled a cigarette, lit up. His eyes narrowed as the smoke curled upwards. 'Beer,' he patiently repeated a second time.

TWENTY-EIGHT

Over the following days Taggart came to know the interior of Manuel's intimately. He lounged at the back table, slowly drinking the luke warm beer until even the locals came to accept him as part of the furnishings. He visited the fort several times in order to give credibility to his story of having come to Sweet Water to discuss the sale of some more horses to the army and he reminded anyone who would listen of his previous dealings in the area.

He listened and he talked, drawing anyone who would join him into conversation. He learned little, except that on the whole Gaze was feared and envied. He had money where money was scarce, he had fine clothes and two horses where poverty was the norm. Personnel at the fort told him of the recent unrest among the Apache tribes, and of the increasing number of braves who somehow had managed to get their hands on a repeater rifle. He called on Lieutenant Washington and his wife, who expressed surprise that they should have the pleasure of a visit so soon. They asked after Lizabeth and sent their warmest regards to her, and the lieutenant discussed in private his concerns that the Indian situation was becoming more serious than at first supposed.

'If things continue as they are now, I shall send Sara back East to her folks until it is sorted out,' he confided.

As the days passed and he made little progress Taggart's patience wore thin. However, just when he was about to give up, Manuel provided him with some pieces of the puzzle, and Gaze finally returned to Sweet Water.

He had spent the greater part of the day as usual occupying the back table, drinking and playing cards. Business had been even slower than usual, and Manuel had joined him. Taggart had encouraged the man to partake of an inordinate quantity of rye whiskey while he himself had sipped carefully at his beer. By that evening Manuel was not exactly drunk, but was certainly in a talkative mood.

'Tell me about this Gaze.' Taggart filled the other man's glass to the brim. '*Salute*,' he said, watching Manuel down the drink in one swallow. Taggart refilled.

Manuel shrugged. 'It is no secret, Señor Taggart, he has powerful friends who take care of him.'

'Take care of him?'

'*Si*, they come whenever.' Again he shrugged. 'They bring many boxes and some whiskey too. Not good whiskey, I have tasted it.' He leaned towards Taggart, and the latter subdued the urge to grimace, catching the other's whiskey-soaked breath. 'Gaze, he thinks we do not know, he thinks we are all fools, but I know. The boxes are hidden in a false bottom of the wagon, and I watch and I listen when the men come. They sell guns I think, to the Indians.' He swayed towards the bottle, and Taggart hastily pushed it within his reach. 'Always there is trouble with the Apache when Gaze returns from doin' the business. They are liquored up and they have more guns.'

Taggart frowned. 'But surely someone at the fort knows 'bout this? Don't they do nothin' 'bout Gaze and his friends?'

Manuel grinned toothlessly. 'They suspect that somethin' is goin' on, but they do nothin'. He comes from a good family. Once they had money and position in these parts, and perhaps the soldiers think that this is still so. He is sly like the fox, that one, he is careful and always he is not caught with boxes.' He broke off suddenly and his eyes widened. There was naked fear on his face and Taggart followed the source of that fear with interest.

'Speak of the Devil,' Manuel said, crossing himself as he pointed towards a young man who had just then walked into the *cantina*. His eyes slid away from Taggart and he swallowed loudly. Taggart ignored him studying Gaze thoughtfully.

The man was as Manuel had led him to expect. From the elaborate, tight charro costume right down to the heavy cartridge belt elegantly scrolled in Mexican silver Gaze spelled ready money. Damn it, he had to be involved in some scheme of Jefferies, he had to!

He rubbed his hand across the back of his neck. Gawd, he was tired. 'I'll have me a beer,' he said aloud. The barkeep scurried to comply. He was so obviously grateful to have escaped further embroilment in Taggart's questioning that Billy almost smiled. Funny how fast fear could sober a man.

It was quite dark when Gaze finally left the *cantina*. He had spent almost the entire day drinking heavily and he was far from sober as he stumbled down the sidewalk. It was easy to follow him. He evidently didn't know of Billy's interest or he was too drunk to care – most likely the latter.

Billy waited about half an hour or so before he approached Gaze's lodgings. A light still showed in the relevant window. Once he saw Gaze's outline silhouetted against the dirty pane. Taggart rolled another cigarette and smoked it slowly while he continued to hold vigil across the street from Gaze's. He had no plan in mind. He figured something would occur to him when the time demanded. For the moment he just waited.

One by one the occupants of Sweet Water quenched their lamps and settled down to slumber. Away in the hills a coyote howled. The night sky was inky-blue, the stars low enough to count. Only the lamp in Gaze's room continued to burn.

Taggart crept closer, coming finally to stand at the foot of the building. He looked upwards to Gaze's lighted window on the second storey and began to climb.

Swinging himself aloft on to the balcony he edged along it, his boots thudding lightly as he crossed the timbers. Peering into Gaze's room, at first he saw nothing. The room appeared to be empty. Taggart frowned.

He had been mistaken in his assumption

that Gaze's lamp still burned at that late hour. It was actually the flickering flames of a fire which burned cheerfully in the grate that lighted the room's interior. Gaze himself was sitting in a chair, his back to the window, his hands stretched out to the flames. The cosy scene framed so invitingly by the window belied the hovel which daylight would reveal so mercilessly.

Taggart drew back. He dropped down again to the hard-packed clay of the street, landing easily and without sound on the balls of his feet.

It was easy to gain access to the building. He found Gaze's room with little difficulty. A thin line of light showed beneath the door, confirming its location. He turned the doorhandle slowly, holding his breath. The door opened with the faintest creak and Taggart was inside the room. Still Gaze did not move. He remained quite still, sitting by the fire, his back to Taggart. He did not turn to give any indication that he was aware of Taggart's presence. Something was wrong, Taggart could feel it but he could not quite put his finger on it exactly.

He slipped his gun from its holster and took maybe three steps forward. He saw the man start, the chair scraped back a little as he began to turn. Hands gripped the arms of the chair, the knuckles showing white in the light emitted by the dying fire. With little darting, scraping movements the man turned the chair until he and Taggart were facing each other.

A log fell in the fire rejuvenating the flames and they leaped upwards into the chimney. In the brief, bright illumination Taggart saw the man's face clearly for the first time. His breath hissed through his teeth.

'What took you so long, Taggart?' Jefferies grinned, his white teeth gleaming in the firelight. He stretched his arms upwards in a lazy way, yawned. He was totally at ease, totally relaxed, totally master of the moment.

TWENTY-NINE

Taggart's gun came up. 'What the hell are you doin' here?' he gritted in a cold voice. 'Ain't that bein' mighty careless of you, Jefferies?' He indicated with his gun that the other man should resume his seat. Jefferies obeyed in silence, but there was a look on his face which Taggart didn't care for. 'Didn't figure on seein' you here in Sweet Water,' he continued, studying the man. 'You bring down the latest deliveries in person?'

Jefferies smiled, but the gesture didn't reach his eyes. 'No,' he replied, spreading his hands wide, 'I haven't come with the latest deliveries, as you put it, I came to find you.' He turned slightly in his chair to glance up at Taggart. 'You thought I wouldn't work it out, that you would come here to Sweet Water. It would appear that Styles's suspicions of Miss FitzMaurice were correct after all. Perhaps he should have slapped her around a little more.' He noticed the tightening of Taggart's mouth with satisfaction. 'Hit a nerve, I see.' He smiled. 'How interesting, the schoolteacher and the dead ex-rancher.'

'Jefferies, you'd best shut up or I may just forget myself and kill you here and now,' Taggart said, tension coiling through him and his grip on the Colt tightening unconsciously.

Jefferies' face lost its smooth calm. 'Don't be a bigger fool than you've already been, Taggart,' he snapped. 'Look behind you.'

Taggart spun round on the balls of his feet. Jaeckell and Styles entered the room even as he pivoted. Jefferies stood up. There was something unpleasant in his expression.

'Damn you,' Taggart muttered beneath his breath and then he was aware of a sickening crunch and the sound of his own groans coming from a long way off. He thought he might throw up.

He felt rough hands drag him from the room and towards the stairs. He jerked backwards in anger, his movements strangely slow and ineffectual. The action sent searing pain through his temple. The room blurred, swirling blackness rushed up to meet him and he fell away into space. There was nothing, nothing at all for quite some time.

Arrowheads of pain shot through his skull as consciousness slowly returned. He was dimly aware of the sway of his body, the smell of horse beneath him and the growing heat of the sun across his back. Gradually he reasoned that his captors were taking him from Sweet Water, heading out into the wilderness. He tried to rouse himself to offer some resistance, but his senses reeled sickeningly. His head thudded against the side of his saddle. He could smell the sand and feel the heavy heat of the desert press in on him and again consciousness slipped from him.

When next he stirred, he was aware that he was lying on the ground. The taste of the desert was in his mouth. At first he thought he had been having the worst kind of nightmare, but even semi-conscious Jaeckell's voice penetrated the fog which clouded his senses.

'Took care of Gaze, boss,' he was saying, the sound of the words coming and going as Taggart strived towards full awareness. 'He ain't gonna be tellin' nobody nothin'.'

'Good, good,' Jefferies' voice replied. 'Can't have liabilities like Gaze hanging round our necks. Bad for business, don't you agree, Mr Jaeckell?'

Jaeckell laughed, the sound grating on Taggart's returning consciousness. Damn, his head hurt. 'What about him?' Jaeckell spoke again.

'I think you deserve that pleasure, Mr Jaeckell,' the latter muttered in dulcet tones. 'I'm quite sure you'll have little difficulty formulating some acceptable plan for disposal of Mr Taggart. Don't you agree, Mr Styles?'

Billy risked a quick glance from half-closed eyes. He'd wondered about the whereabouts of Styles.

Styles held himself at a distance from the other two men. He did not immediately acknowledge Jefferies' observation, but eyed him with his personal brand of speculation. There was a slightly wary look on his face.

'Can't we just do this and be done with it?' he bit out impatiently. For a moment he regarded Jefferies with unnerving steadiness. 'Killin' a man, that's one thing,' he said at last, 'but what you've got planned, hell, that ain't civilized.'

'Precisely,' Jefferies responded at once in an eager kind of way. 'This must look as if it is the work of Indians.' He paused, a wolfish grin on his lips. 'Besides,' he continued, an unmistakable thread of irony beneath the words, 'Jaeckell here is so looking forward to it.' He gestured wildly in Taggart's general direction. 'He is the key to all my plans. That damn valley is more difficult to take than I had anticipated, but once news of Taggart's demise reaches Boonetown, I think Jim Taylor will begin to see sense.' He shrugged in a careless fashion. 'There is, of course, also the faint possibility that he had indeed learned something of value to bring back to Tom Lawson. I can't allow that possibility to mature. You do understand the difficulty which faces me, I am sure, Mr

Styles? However, I digress...' He paused for a moment, a tight frown creasing his face. 'Paint him in mesquite juice,' he gritted then with tense impatience.

'Why not just get rid of Lawson, boss?' Jaeckell grunted, busily pushing Taggart around just for the pleasure it afforded him.

Jefferies swung towards the speaker. 'Don't be a bigger fool than you usually are, Jaeckell,' he spat out in biting tones. 'Kill a lawman and bring all kinds of investigations to Boonetown, are you mad?' He drew a steadying breath, smoothed his hair and replaced his hat at a very precise angle. 'Leave him for the ants,' he instructed, glancing with distaste at Taggart. 'A horrible end I do agree,' he directed this towards Styles, 'but richly deserved in this particular instance. I must say, the prospect just makes this whole day perfect.' He rubbed his hands together as if washing them. 'Yes, indeed,' he repeated, 'yes, indeed.'

He laughed, the sound devoid of humour. There was a madness about him in those moments, something evil and out of control. 'Assist him, Mr Styles,' Jefferies added, in a hard tone, turning suddenly towards the latter.

Styles held his ground, his stance stub-

215

born. 'Jaeckell can manage,' he replied, after some moments had passed, 'don't need no help.'

Billy made a gallant attempt to escape but was easily foiled. Nevertheless he continued to struggle as Jaeckell, finally assisted by a scowling Styles, tied him spreadeagled between four stakes hammered into the desert floor. The sticky, rather sweet-tasting mesquite juice dripped down his face into his mouth. He spat weakly, twisting his head from side to side.

The sun shone down mercilessly, a great ball of fire in the wide, cloudless sky. He fancied he saw that same hunting hawk hovering just overhead and somewhere inside him anger, like a palpable force, erupted. He pulled fiercely against his bonds. 'I'll kill you,' he bellowed, ''fore Gawd, I'll kill you, you hear me, Jefferies?' Jefferies came to stand by Taggart's head. Taggart's eyes were just level with the toe of the other's dusty leather boots. He glanced upwards, squinting into the full glare of the sun overhead.

'Kill me?' I don't think so, Mr Taggart.' He hunched down, Indian fashion, bending so close to Taggart's face that the latter could feel his breath brush his cheek. 'You can't imagine the pleasure this gives me,' he said softly. Again that grin with just that faint hint of madness. 'Did you really think that you would defeat me? You, with your honour and your principles and your damn loyalty?' He stood up then, his face kind of hard and rather pale. 'I'll take your valley, you'll see, I'll take it and destroy it, just to best you, you fool.' He straightened, assuming a grave expression. 'Firstly, however, I have the unhappy task of informing all concerned of your unfortunate death at the hands of savages. I may even be called upon to say something at your memorial service.' He laughed with genuine amusement. 'How absolutely priceless.'

He gestured that Jaeckell should fetch the horses, tethered perhaps six yards away. 'Goodbye, Mr Taggart,' he said as he mounted, 'it's been an education.'

Billy stretched his head round as far as his bonds would allow and watched the riders leave. He was alone finally and in trouble so deep he wasn't sure he'd ever surface. Wouldn't take long for the ant telegraph to get wind of his predicament. One bite meant nothing, a few was uncomfortable, thousands meant almost certain death.

Immediately he set to work on the ropes

binding him. The moments passed, becoming hours. Sweat beaded his face. His lips cracked painfully in the sun. He'd managed at last, with considerable difficulty to slightly loosen the bonds on his left hand. His wrists were bleeding from constant rubbing against the ropes, but he hardly noticed. He wiped his dry tongue across his lips and kept twisting his wrists in an effort to further free his hands.

Preoccupied as he was, it was some time before he became aware of the faint persistent movement of the sand off to his right. His breath caught in his throat. From the corner of his eye he saw the approach of the first of the ant regiments. He dragged desperately at the stakes. Perhaps he could pull one up. They were driven deep and solid, it was hopeless. He hadn't a chance in hell!

He couldn't keep his eyes off the approaching ants. They seemed to mesmerize him, hypnotize him. He could feel the colony crawl on to his legs, his chest, like a black plague, on to his face, into his mouth. He spat, twisting his head madly. A pulse throbbed in his throat and his heart began to pound.

In his blackest moment he began to

hallucinate. Somewhere in his head there was a strangely persistent pounding, a rhythm reminiscent of drums beating. He fancied again that the hawk hovered over his head, watching and waiting for its prey. Its beak dripping red with blood, and its eyes were black and pitiless. A creature squealed. Taggart heard it. He couldn't be sure it wasn't himself!

THIRTY

For a time he fought the black dreaming, and then allowed himself to sink into it as the only escape open to him. He glanced upwards into the sun and thought he saw Lizabeth's face smiling at him. He wanted to reach out, but didn't. He fancied he heard her call his name.

'Here,' he yelled and no sound came. 'Here,' he tried a second time, his voice a mere croak, barely audible. 'Taggart,' he imagined a disembodied voice saying. Someone bent and severed the ropes binding him. He was hoisted upright. A dribble of water was allowed into his mouth, while rough hands brushed briskly at the ants and dragged desperately at his clothes. He reached towards the source of the water but it was too far away, in another world, another place.

He could see the valley then in his mind's eye. It was summer and the meadows were still decked with flowers, the lake shone, beckoning in the sunshine. He dipped his hand into the refreshing depths and drank. It was sweet as wild honey. He thought he opened his eyes, but he wasn't sure. The sun hurt too much, and the pit beckoned. He felt himself falling into the blackness. It was cool there, and rather pleasant. Someone wiped his mouth and face with something cold and bitter. He twisted away, shook his head. He heard someone moan and didn't recognize the sound of his own voice. And then there was nothing. He no longer dreamed and he no longer saw the valley. There was only the black, bottomless pit, and the hawk hovering.

It was almost two days and nights before Taggart was again aware of his surroundings. He didn't move at all when he first opened his eyes, just looked around him. He was so surprised to find himself still alive that it took him some time to assimilate the fact. After a time, he became aware that he was lying on a low pallet, covered lightly by a single blanket. He raised himself with effort on to his arm, and glanced around.

A small fire burned in the centre of the tepee, the smoke curling upwards in a thin, lazy stream towards the smoke hole above. Several blankets, similar to the one covering him were stacked on the floor close by, and he presumed that whoever was responsible for his recovery had used them to insulate him from the night's cold.

He swung his legs to the side of the pallet, his head swimming. He sat there for a time until he felt better and then pushed himself to his feet, swaying a little. There were several bowls and various other possessions scattered about the tepee, some hanging from poles. In the far corner he spotted a drinking gourd full of water and dipped the carved wooden cup into it with something akin to desperation. As he was dipping the cup for the third time, the flap of the tepee was pushed aside. Taggart swung round.

Recognizing the small figure who was on the point of entry, Taggart called out, 'Little Bear ... where am...' The boy, however, merely studied him in silence for some moments and then spun on his heels and disappeared. 'Damn,' Taggart muttered. He had just returned the drinking cup to its original position by the water gourd when the tent flap was once again pushed aside. This time, the man entering paused to tie it back, leaving an opening through which the sunshine poured into the interior. He stood in the open flap, looking outwards, saying nothing.

Taggart after a moment's pause, went to join Black Eagle by the opening. Outside, dogs wandered around, scrabbling for scraps, fighting among themselves. He could see pots bubbling over open fires and his stomach rumbled as the scent of cooking meat reached him.

'You are hungry?' Black Eagle enquired, as if reading his mind.

'A little,' Taggart agreed, not wishing to appear too eager. Black Eagle gestured to a young squaw who was hovering close by. She glanced shyly at Taggart and then scurried quickly to prepare a meal for him as Black Eagle had commanded.

'How long have I been here?' Taggart asked, turning to comply with the chief's request that he return to his pallet. He did so gladly, more weakened than he had anticipated by the brief exertion.

'Two days and nights,' Black Eagle replied, 'you had a bad fever. You were very ill. I did not think you would see another sunrise, but we have medicine which make you well.' Taggart closed his eyes for a moment.

'Medicine?' he queried, in a sleepy voice.

'Herbs, roots.' Black Eagle shrugged his shoulders off-handedly. 'The wise men among us know of such things. They know the magic and the old ways...' His voice faded away and Taggart slept. He never did eat that particular meal prepared so efficiently by the little squaw.

But he ate with relish the breakfast she prepared the following morning. He had never been so hungry. He felt stronger too and almost his old self. Having completed his meal, he amused himself by watching the comings and goings about camp. He was aware that he himself was something of an attraction, a novelty, especially for the children. Several groups approached, giggling and obviously nervous only to scatter screaming when he ventured to speak to them.

He wondered where Black Eagle was that morning. It somehow surprised him that the chief had not come to visit, but he learned indirectly from an overheard conversation that he had gone out with a hunting party many hours before sun-up. He had apparently not yet returned.

As the morning passed and Black Eagle still had not returned, Taggart became a little uneasy. He had noticed many of the younger braves glance towards him and there was something obstinate and vehement about their faces. 'It's your hair,' Little Bear enlightened him with something very like glee. 'The braves have never seen hair with so much moonlight in it.' He squatted down with difficulty beside Taggart, his broken arm outstretched. 'It would bring good fortune, I am thinking, a great coup to take your hair,' he continued in a friendly fashion.

'I am kinda partial to keepin' my hair where it is,' Taggart rejoined in a dry voice, glancing at his young companion. 'Your father has not returned?' Little Bear grinned and Taggart noticed that the boy had lost two front teeth since their last meeting.

'If the hunting goes well, he will soon return, if not, it will take longer.' For some time the two sat in silence. The children, tired of studying the strange paleface were playing noisily some distance away, among the rocks.

'Soon I will go with the hunt,' Little Bear

said with satisfaction. 'Although my father says I must wait at least another summer, I am no longer a child to play foolish games among the rocks.'

'And your arm, it is mending?'

The boy shifted a little, seeking a more comfortable position. 'It hurts sometimes,' he admitted reluctantly, glancing down at the offending limb with enmity. 'It keeps me from the hunt.' He bit his lip. 'My father is pleased with you, Taggart. He had told the braves that you must not be harmed. It is his wish.'

Taggart shrugged lazily. 'That's good to know,' he said. The boy continued to stare fixedly at a point just above his companion's head. Taggart merely closed his eyes.

'The men who left you for the ants, you knew them, they were your friends?'

'Not what I'd call friends exactly,' Taggart said, a thread of irony in the words, 'acquaintances more like.'

Little Bear looked up, genuinely puzzled. 'Acquaintances?' he repeated the unfamiliar word with difficulty.

'Definitely not friends,' Taggart continued.

The boy's face cleared. 'They were your enemies?'

'Taggart ran his fingers through his hair,

turning his face up towards the sun. 'I reckon you could say that,' he agreed lazily, not really interested.

'My father intends to honour you, he has said he will kill your enemies. That is good, yes?' Taggart's eyes snapped open, his head pivoting round to stare at the boy.

'Kill my enemies?' he repeated.

The boy nodded. 'It is my father's wish,' he said, with something akin to pride. 'I hear him talk of it when he thought I was asleep. He called you his brother, Taggart; your enemies are his enemies, that is our way.' Little Bear twisted to look into Taggart's face. 'You are not pleased?' he said doubtfully.

For a long moment Taggart was silent. 'Your enemies are my enemies,' he muttered beneath his breath, the implications endless. 'Yes,' he said aloud, 'I am pleased.'

During the following days Taggart regained his strength. He no longer grew tired at the least exertion, and the recurring headaches which the shaman had treated with some concoction of Indian turnip, gradually came at longer intervals. With the rapid return of vigour his desire to leave the village increased and he watched for the return of Black Eagle with increasingly impatient eagerness.

There was much whooping when Black Eagle's party finally returned. The whole camp was flung into a vortex of activity. The hunting had gone well and the camp-fires would burn brightly that evening, the cooking pots bubbling with promise. However, while the camp might gorge itself that day, there would be lean months to follow and accordingly, meat was preserved by cutting it into thin slices and hanging it out to dry. The squaws started working on the hides almost immediately, pegging them on the ground. They worked on the exposed side, removing fat and meat with a flesher.

Little Bear had been showing Taggart how to make a bow. At sight of the incoming party, he had leaped to his feet, his face bright with excitement and gladness, the carefully selected ash discarded at his feet. 'My father, he is come,' he stated the obvious, pointing towards Black Eagle who sat his horse not six feet from where they had sat. The chief studied him not even blinking, his expression penetrating and fearless, the face of a proud warrior.

Taggart stood up. He raised his hand in the traditional greeting, but made no movement forward. Black Eagle merely nodded. Taggart watched in silence as the hot-blooded braves continued to circle the camp, whooping and waving their weapons above their heads. One dared to ride quite close to Taggart, touching him with his coupstick.

'Enough,' Black Eagle bellowed, and the young warrior pulled his pony away in a tight circle, obedient but defiant. 'Come.' Black Eagle slipped easily to the ground, waiting while Taggart fell into step beside him. 'It is perhaps time that we spoke of your leaving. The warriors grow restless, especially now, having counted coup on their enemies. We took many horses, that is good.' He broke off watching Little Bear hurtling across the camp, his face shining with discovery.

THIRTY-ONE

'Your horse,' he said to Taggart in a breathless rush, 'it is by the stream.'

Taggart glanced at him in surprise. He had last seen the grey being led away by Jaeckell. 'It is?' he replied dubiously.

'Some of the warriors, they brought him

228

into camp. They did not know that he was your horse, but I knew him. I told them that my father would wish that he be returned to you.' He glanced up at Taggart, a sly look on his face. 'It is true that white men value their horse above all else?' he queried.

'Reckon so,' Taggart agreed good-naturedly, 'we depend on 'em.' He glanced at Black Eagle, who indicated that they should both follow Little Bear and see this horse of Taggart's.

'Sometimes we eat our horses,' Little Bear continued matter-of-factly, keeping up with the men's long strides with some difficulty. Taggart merely grunted.

The grey, recognizing Taggart, whinnied, blowing softly through his nose. He came forward and nuzzled the man. Taggart ran his hand down the gelding's neck and spoke gently. He walked the gelding a little, checking him over, relieved to find that there was nothing wrong that a good feed wouldn't cure. To Taggart's further surprise his saddle was still on the grey, his gunbelt slung around its horn. Black Eagle watched him, but said nothing as Taggart circled his hips with the familiar weight of his belt, spun the chamber and settled his gun into its holster.

'The raid brought many horses,' he said in his guttural voice, indicating the other horses which the warriors were even then dividing. 'I claim that one for myself, it is a horse worthy of a chief.'

The bay stallion in question was known to Taggart. He had seen Jefferies ride him on too many occasions to be mistaken now. 'The man who rode him, is he here?' he said, keeping the tension from his voice with difficulty.

Black Eagle shrugged. 'He is dead,' he said flatly. 'My warriors count coup. It is the way of battle, is it not?' For a moment Taggart thought on that, but only one thought was spinning round in his head as he looked at Jefferies' big bay stallion that day. He could feel all the shattered pieces come together in that moment. He was conscious suddenly of a great weight lifting, of a physical and mental gladness which went right to the core of him. He sighed and closed his eyes against the glare of that too big sun.

It was over. He could go home. It was finally time to go home.

For some strange reason, Taggart expected that the valley would have changed somehow in his absence. It surprised him then that on his return he found it looked exactly as he remembered.

The mountains still continued to dominate the scene, still loomed peaceful and eternal above the green graze and the pine belt. The meadows were still decked with summer flowers, and that came as something of a shock too. With all that had happened to him during the previous weeks, he had imagined summer to have ended. Atop the South Pass, now unguarded, he reined in the grey and dismounted.

He stood there for a long time, very quiet and still. He was not really thinking of anything, just savouring the moment. The air he found still carried that distinctive scent of pines.

He had ridden out directly from town, having first taken time to have a much needed bath and shave. His long discussion with a pleased Tom Lawson had put his mind at rest concerning a lot of things, and he had whistled cheerfully as he and the grey had taken the road from Boonetown to the ranch. Lawson reckoned that the bank might even see fit to make some new arrangements with Zack Hale considering the circumstances surrounding Jefferies' acquisition of the Hale spread. 'That should please ole Zack,' he figured aloud, 'when I tell 'im.' He bent forward to rub the grey's soft ears through his fingers. The gelding snorted with pleasure.

All that remained of Jefferies' bid for the valley was the dead ashes of several camp-fires which spotted the base of the pass. It seemed to Taggart as he rode past that Lawson was proving right in that respect too. Deprived of their driving force, and with no wages forthcoming, the bid for the valley had fallen apart. One moment, Taylor explained later, they were there, the next they had just upped and ridden out.

Taggart finally came down into the valley, riding slowly through the upper meadows. He noticed with pleasure how well the grass had sprung up in the interim. It seemed a long time to him then since he and the others had eaten together in the hay field. He circled the lake remembering how it had looked to him in his feverish dreams. He finally came upon the ranch complex by way of the lower grazing pastures. Smoke streamed from the kitchen chimney and Jesse's hens scrabbled as always for titbits in the yard. Nothing, at least on the surface, had changed.

It was obvious that someone had been

posted to watch for him. He was still some distance from the house when the door was flung open and all those who were evidently waiting to welcome him home, emerged. The menfolk contented themselves with a dignified advance, the ladies waited in the porch overhang. Jesse, however, came to meet him at full gallop. She tripped in her haste, picking herself up quickly, hardly seeming to notice. Taggart knee'd the grey to a canter and the horse ate up the distance between them, finally coming abreast of the racing Jesse. He dismounted hastily and she flung herself into his arms. 'You're alive, you're alive,' she repeated over and over. 'We heard you was dead.' He held her tightly, feeling the smallness of her, the warmth of her and he knew at last that peace had returned to the valley.

He shook hands with the men, told Zack the good news concerning his ranch and was ushered inside to enjoy a positive feast which had been prepared in honour of his safe return. During the course of the day he repeated his adventures more times than he cared to count for the benefit of his friends. All the while, however, he was conscious of Lizabeth, how pretty she was and how much he had looked forward to seeing her again.

That evening, when all the celebrations had abated, Zack announced that he and his boys were hankering to go home. They were all packed and ready. Wasn't no reason not to leave at first light the following morning. It wasn't that he didn't appreciate Taylor's offer to stay a mite longer, he explained earnestly, but he sure had him a hankering to sleep in his own bed. It was only a matter of time, he reckoned, before the whole business was settled. Meantime, there were chores needing doing round the place; the longer he was gone, the more there was to do.

Rosa Lee too was anxious to return to civilization as she put it. She was tired of the rustic life and positively yearned for bright lights, music and noise. It was so damn quiet, she complained, out here in the middle of nowhere that it kept her awake most nights. 'I'm leavin' first thing in the mornin' with Zack and the boys,' she announced to no one in particular. 'Lizabeth can come along too,' she added generously. 'Nothin' keepin' you here is there, now that all's back to normal.'

Lizabeth had been sewing some buttons on to a shirt of Taylor's, her head bent over the work. She kept her face averted. 'No,' she said very softly, a little sadly, 'there isn't anything to keep me here now.' She put her work aside then with a thoughtful air. 'I think I'll take a little walk before I turn in,' she said looking up. 'Please excuse me.'

Taggart watched her leave, standing silhouetted in the window while she crossed the yard outside. She was heading for the barn. His eyes followed her eagerly etching the image of her tall, slender figure and the long raven-black hair on to his sub-conscious. She was leaving in the morning and he might never see her again. Somehow that twisted round his heart.

'Go after her, you fool,' Jesse whispered fiercely. 'Go on,' she pushed him towards the door as she spoke and he went willingly, needing only token encouragement. Lizabeth threw him an uneasy glance as he fell into step alongside her. They strolled in silence for some time, the dusk drawing in to the valley seeming to hold its breath as if waiting.

'It's very beautiful, isn't it.' Lizabeth said rather wistfully. She paused to gaze upwards towards the mountains where the last fingers of daylight still clung. 'I shall miss it all a great deal when I leave.'

She shivered, wrapping her arms around

herself. Taggart stood very close to her, not touching but she felt as if he had. The scent of bay rum aftershave stirred her senses, and she sighed, something somewhere inside her aching with longing.

'When are you thinkin' of leavin',' he said, his breath touching her cheek. She did not move, could not, even had she wanted to.

'Soon,' she replied in a husky voice. 'Perhaps I might take Rosa up on her offer and leave in the morning.'

He kicked the toe of one dusty boot against a stone, pushing his hands deeply into the levis pockets. 'That soon.'

She turned then and there was something in her face which caused him to draw his breath in sharply. 'There isn't anything, or...' she paused, 'anyone, to keep me here, is there, Billy?' He didn't immediately look away and she saw his expression grow pensive. The evocative hush of the darkening valley wrapped round them, whispering soft nothings, transient as an angel's wing brushing against their skin.

'We'll sure miss you,' he said. Lizabeth turned away so that all he saw was the back of her head and the moonlight shining silver in her hair. 'I'll miss you,' he amended softly. Still she did not turn. 'I'll miss you,' he repeated. The silence which followed his words lengthened and took on a life of its own. It pulsated with emotion, with misunderstanding, with regret, with desire, perhaps even with love.

'Why,' she said in a fierce voice, 'do you imagine I came out here in the first place? Why,' – she stopped, her breath hissing through her teeth, – 'do you think I'm leaving now? Do you think I came all this way just so I can hear you say that you'll miss me?' Billy drew back a step, startled by the strength of her anger. He pulled his hands awkwardly from his pockets, spread them out, palms upwards.

'Hell, Liz,' he muttered, 'I ain't never known what's what where you're concerned, now ain't no different.'

'Damn it, Billy,' she gritted impatiently, practically stamping her foot. 'This isn't the time for jesting.'

He met her eyes. 'Who's jestin'?' he replied faintly, at a loss as to how he should proceed in the face of her obvious hostility.

'Ah, to hell with this,' she burst out, 'the hell with you.' She pivoted suddenly. 'Damn, damn, damn,' he heard her muttering as she quickened her steps until she was almost running.

'Lizabeth,' his voice halted her flight and she could hear his step behind her. She paused, her head bent as he came to stand by her.

This time he did touch her. His hands were warm on her bare skin and she shivered as his fingers curved round the soft flesh of her upper arms.

'Don't go in the mornin',' he said, not knowing what else he should say. Still she averted her head, a stubborn tilt to her chin.

'Don't go,' he continued. She waited. 'I want you to stay, you know I want you to stay. Damn it, I don't ever want you to go. I love you, you fool female.'

'Damn it,' she whispered, mocking him gently, her eyes shining as she turned into the circle of his arms. 'It took you long enough.'

This Large Print Book, for people
who cannot read normal print,
is published under the auspices of

THE ULVERSCROFT FOUNDATION